"I don't know what to say, Alex."

Gail reached for the roses Alex was offering. Was it really proper, she wondered, to thank him for bringing flowers to the woman he knew as his best friend's fiancée?

"Don't say anything. Maybe I should just show you why I came." Alex's big hand covered hers on the back of the chair. As he bent and touched his lips briefly to hers, Gail felt a sudden dizziness.

"Oh, Alex," she murmured, her mind reeling. Who was she? Gail? Monica? Had she completely lost her sanity and become both herself and her twin sister?

Suddenly, she stepped off the tightrope she had been walking for days. She was Gail, and she knew what she wanted.

She wanted Alex....

ABOUT THE AUTHOR

Kaye Walton is the pseudonym for the writing team of Lois Carnell and Sandra Dark. Both authors live in Norman, Oklahoma. Sandra has written numerous magazine articles and short stories, and Lois has published a number of romance novels and short stories.

Although the two met through writers' organizations, they had not considered working together until, as Sandra says, "We both needed a change of pace, so we teamed up. *Over the Horizon* is their first Superromance novel. Their second will be out next year.

Over the Horizon

KAYE WALTON

Harlequin Books

TORONTO • NEW YORK • LONDON
AMSTERDAM • PARIS • SYDNEY • HAMBURG
STOCKHOLM • ATHENS • TOKYO • MILAN

Published December 1991

ISBN 0-373-70479-8

OVER THE HORIZON

To Bill, with love and appreciation,
for test-flying the Shadow

CHAPTER ONE

A NOXIOUS MANTLE of smog hung over Los Angeles. Gail Montgomery had taken only a few steps when she began to feel the corrosive air burning her lungs. Coupled with that was a strange, spine-tingling sensation that she was being followed.

She dismissed the thought and picked up her pace, causing her sling purse to swing at her side. Thanks to Dr. Calcutt, she was already pressed for time. If she was late, she could count on Alicia Temple to turn their long-standing lunch date into a lecture on time management.

The Venetian Room was six blocks from Gail's office. Halfway there, the chilling sensation returned, this time with a vengeance. Her heart skipped a beat, and she wondered if overwork could be driving her toward some kind of anxiety attack. Or if it had to do with the mysterious meeting that Dr. Calcutt had set up for her at one-thirty. It just wasn't like Calcutt to be so secretive.

Gail stopped before a tiny boutique on busy Los Angeles Boulevard, pretending interest in a flame red linen sundress. Her quick inspection of the unfamiliar passersby reflected in the window glass did little to reassure her, even though no one seemed particularly interested in her. She turned her head sharply and saw two men halt abruptly near the corner. Gail watched them for a moment as they stood talking to each other.

"Kiddo, your mind is going," she murmured to herself. Yet the strange apprehension remained with her as she strode at a faster clip toward the Venetian Room.

She couldn't afford to let the pressure get to her now that Martindale Aircraft's fuel injection project had been approved. Thanks to her own innovative design, she had been named chief project engineer. Besides her justifiable pride in that achievement, she had to admit to more than a little nervousness that she might somehow blow her first big break.

By the time she neared the entrance to the Venetian Room, Gail had managed to put aside the thought that she was being stalked. The September smog had grabbed her total attention. She pushed through the restaurant's double glass doors, yearning for a breath of clean country air.

"What on earth?" Alicia rose from a velvet-cushioned bench in the ornate vestibule, her usually pert face bunched with concern. "You look as if you're being chased by a man-eating shark."

Gail managed a dry laugh. Alicia's exaggerations had a way of deflating Gail's anxieties. Maybe that was part of what made them such good friends.

"The only thing chasing me is my overactive imagination," she said, and smiled at Alicia's puzzled expression. "Lead on. I'm famished."

She followed Alicia to a table and sank into a wicker chair facing the room. A moment later she glanced up from her menu as the two men she had spotted near the boutique entered. They settled at a distant table without so much as glancing in her direction.

"Who are they?" Alicia asked, following her gaze.

"Nobody," Gail said with conviction. "Just a couple of fellow hungry souls."

"The short one's kind of cute." Alicia eyed them speculatively. "Why don't you vamp on over there and put your sexy, smoky-eyed rocket scientist move on him? Maybe they'll join us."

Gail groaned and picked up her menu. "I don't work on rockets, and I'm certainly not sexy," she murmured. The fact was, she had felt ugly as a warthog for months.

Alicia snapped up her own menu. "That jerk you were going with just left you with a bad emotional flash burn, that's all," she said, as if reading Gail's mind.

"Cliff wasn't that bad," Gail protested, knowing that she wasn't convincing her friend.

"Then why did you turn into a manic workaholic after the slug walked out on you?"

"You're blowing it out of proportion," Gail retorted, yielding more ground. "You ought to stick with script writing. You don't have a license to practice psychology."

"Maybe not," Alicia said with a wicked grin. "But if I'm all that far off target, why are you squirming in your chair?"

"It has nothing to do with Cliff," Gail maintained, annoyed that her own body language was giving her away. "I'm just in a rush. Dr. Calcutt arranged a one-thirty meeting with a couple of strangers that I don't have time to fool with."

Alicia put down her menu and squinted at her with suspicious concern. "That isn't all of it, Gail. What's really bothering you?"

Gail sighed. "I don't know, Alicia. It's probably just my imagination, but Dr. Calcutt seemed so evasive about the meeting—almost as if he were trying to lay the groundwork for something unpleasant. I have a horrible feeling that he might be dissatisfied with my work."

Alicia snorted. "Fat chance. Besides, I thought the old guy had the hots for you."

"That is not funny," Gail said coldly.

"Sorry. A bad choice of words." Alicia made a sweeping motion with one hand, as if to erase what she had just said. "Still, he wouldn't pull the project out from under you, would he?"

Gail's stomach heaved at the thought. Now twenty-nine years old, she had never failed at anything—with the glaring exception of her relationship with Cliff Danvers. But however hard she tried to deny it, that disaster had left her self-esteem shaken to its foundations.

Alicia was dead right about one thing: Gail had been using work as an antidote. The simple truth was that if she slowed down now, before the cure was complete, she might very well crack up.

Her gaze drifted aimlessly across the room. When it settled on the table where the two men had been sitting, Gail felt an inexplicable chill. The table was empty.

AT PRECISELY ONE-THIRTY, Gail stood at the door to her office. Before entering, she paused to run her fingers over the new gold lettering that had been applied just that morning. G. Montgomery, Chief, Jet Propulsion. A sense of pride accompanied her through the doorway into the large, sparsely furnished room. She halted, one hand still on the doorknob, when she realized that her office was already occupied.

Abney Calcutt stopped pacing the middle of the room and turned as she entered. His hazel eyes peered kindly from a face that was weathered and wrinkled from exposure to the desert sun.

During her years at Martindale, Gail had come to regard Dr. Calcutt not only as a father figure but also a much-appreciated mentor. She was grateful for the large part he had played in helping her achieve her current status. But right now, his worried expression made her very uneasy.

She looked past him at the two other men standing with their backs to the door, studying the decidedly unspectacular view from the unadorned office window. When they turned to face her, Gail could only gape at them. They were the same two she had seen on the street near the boutique and again at the Venetian Room.

As she came into the room and closed the door, Gail searched Calcutt's face for an explanation and saw his frown deepen. He came over and placed a hand upon her shoulder, as if sympathizing with her. The gesture further confused Gail. She felt as though she had walked in on a jury that had been deliberating her fate—for a crime she didn't know she had committed.

"Gail, I'm going to leave you alone with these gentlemen," Calcutt said, without bothering to make introductions. "Please come to my office when you're finished."

He squeezed her shoulder, and she had a distinct impression that he was reluctant to leave her. But he did, moving quickly to the door. When he was gone, Gail turned her attention to the two strangers.

"Good afternoon, Ms. Montgomery," the shorter of the two men said, striking toward her. An exaggeratedly wholesome smile creased his round, freckled face, his youthful appearance accentuated by a healthy crop of sandy hair. "Name's Dick Brady. And this is Howard Eastman."

He indicated his older companion, a distinguished-looking, white-haired man of about fifty. Eastman remained near the window as Brady whipped out a card case and held up his identification for Gail to inspect.

"I'm with the National Security Agency," Brady said. "Mr. Eastman is with Defense Intelligence."

Gail stared at them for another moment, then motioned both men toward chairs. She circled her desk, instinctively wanting to put a chunk of furniture between the two visitors and herself. What on earth did they want with her?

"We appreciate your taking the time to meet with us," Eastman said diplomatically, in a well-modulated voice bearing just a trace of a Southern drawl. He leaned forward slightly, studying her intently, as if examining every line and contour of her face. "Were you aware that Dick and I followed you to your luncheon engagement?"

Gail nodded apprehensively.

"She's very observant," Eastman said to Brady, clearly pleased. "That will certainly come in handy."

"She's also an incredible carbon copy," Brady noted. "Change the hairdo, and we could be in business."

Gail's eyebrows rose as Eastman nodded. Impatience and curiosity were beginning to override her confusion. In the space of two minutes she had developed an uncomfortably enlightened awareness of how it felt to be a laboratory animal.

"What can I do for you gentlemen?" she asked bluntly, trying to gain a foothold in the one-sided conversation.

"Infinitely more than you can imagine," Brady said with a disarming smile. "For starters, we want you to work for us."

Gail looked from Brady to Eastman and back again. "Is this some kind of hoax?" she asked. Gail had an extremely low tolerance for practical jokes.

Brady's smile widened. "How prescient of you, Ms. Montgomery. As a matter of fact, we're here to persuade you to *perpetrate* a hoax." His smile vanished, as if he had thrown a switch. "It's a matter of grave national security."

Definitely a joke. Gail straightened in her chair, drawing her lips to a thin line. She couldn't believe Dr. Calcutt would be a party to making her the butt of someone's sick humor.

Was he reading her mind? Eastman hastily reached into his inside coat pocket and produced a manila envelope, which he slid across the desk to her. Gail hesitated, then opened it. She slid a snapshot onto her desk blotter and stared at her own face.

Just the face is mine, she thought, startled. The clothes were unfamiliar, as was the small segment of what appeared to be a living room that showed in the background. *The face.* It held her attention for a long moment, like a hypnotist's talisman. Then she blinked and looked at Eastman. The joke was elaborate— she'd give it that.

"It's amazing what can be done in darkrooms these days," she said, pleased with herself for having figured it out so quickly. "But as an example of trick photography, I don't think it holds a candle to *Roger Rabbit.*"

Neither man seemed amused. Gail certainly was not. Brady cleared his throat.

"You have every reason to be confused, Ms. Montgomery," he said, choosing the words carefully. "You see, this is not a doctored photo of you." He paused, as if for effect, and then said, "The woman is Monica Seabury, who happens to be your twin sister.''

Gail almost laughed. She rose from her chair instead, clutching the picture, and walked to the window for a closer look. They were pulling her leg. They had to be. She tilted the snapshot toward the window light and studied it carefully.

There were the same smoky-blue eyes, with the faint gray shadow above that enhanced the translucent color. The same full lower lip and well-defined upper, and the same chestnut-colored hair—the latter styled shorter than Gail's. The clincher was the pert, upturned nose.

Gail scrutinized the photo, certain that she was examining her own image. And yet . . . she shivered, her hands suddenly trembling. When she finally moved back to her desk, she found that her legs had turned to rubber. She sagged into her chair, leaning on the desk for support.

Somewhere in the deepest recesses of her mind, Gail recalled the elusive awareness that she had often experienced while growing up—a sense that she was not completely whole. Now a tiny thrill edged its way into her consciousness. *Had she known all along that she was a twin?*

All those growing-up years, knowing she was adopted, yet not being told who she was or where she had been born, had left a strange void in her life. A void that a stunningly powerful mixture of emotions now struggled to fill.

"This can't be," she said, a part of her still resisting such an astounding possibility.

"It *is*," Eastman said firmly. "If you require further proof beyond that photo, you will be provided with genetic test results, in addition to the sealed adoption records from the Kentucky child welfare office. I might add that your sister reacted with identical disbelief when we told her last week."

"But Monica didn't mention *Roger Rabbit*," Brady pointed out, smiling again.

Gail continued to stare at the snapshot with a deepening sense of connection. She fled back in time, as though a screen were being lifted from her memory. After her adoption at the age of two, she had "manufactured" a sister—a comforting likeness of herself. As she'd grown older, however, the fabricated sibling had faded, its existence all but forgotten until this moment. For the first time, Gail now realized that her sister hadn't been just an eccentric fantasy of an only child.

A wave of curiosity overcame her skepticism. "Where is she? What is she like? When can I see her?"

"Monica looks and sounds exactly like you, as far as we can tell," Brady said, with Eastman nodding agreement. "As for when you can meet her—there is a complication. You see, Monica has disappeared."

"Disappeared?" Gail exclaimed, stung by disappointment. "What do you mean?"

Brady shifted in his chair and frowned at Eastman. Again selecting his words carefully, he said, "We'll get to that, Ms. Montgomery. But first, I must caution you that what we are about to discuss is a matter of national security and must not leave this room."

"My current work involves a government contract," Gail said, certain they already knew. "I have a midlevel security clearance."

Brady nodded. "As a matter of fact, that's how we discovered the biological link between you and Monica. When your background information for your security clearance was being routinely cross-checked in Washington three years ago, the computer kicked out Monica's file."

"Three years ago?" she repeated, astonished. "You knew about Monica and me all this time, and nobody bothered to tell either of us?"

"You must understand the information was highly confidential," Brady said. "Under normal circumstances, we still wouldn't be at liberty to divulge it."

Gail met his steady gaze for a moment. His explanation was reasonable, yet it gave her no satisfaction. "Let's be frank, Mr. Brady," she said, losing patience. "You didn't come here just to deliver the news that I have a twin. How about laying some of *your* cards on the table? Such as why the computer kicked out Monica's file. What kind of work does she do, anyway? And does that have something to do with her disappearance?"

Brady leaned forward, plainly gathering his thoughts. "Monica has worked for us, off and on, for nearly five years," he said finally.

Gail sat up straighter, distinctly aware that Eastman was not happy with what Brady had just told her. But Brady barely glanced at him before forging on.

"Let me explain first that, besides being twins, your career choices show some remarkable similarities—although Monica's tends more toward administration than science. Working from the inside, she has been very helpful to us in situations where we suspect fraud or other irregularities involving various government contractors. Her accounting and administrative analysis expertise parallels your engineering genius."

"Are you saying that Monica works undercover?" Gail asked, strumming her fingers on the desk. "My sister is a spy?"

Brady tilted his head diagonally—apparently a conditional nod. "Monica is a legitimate, experienced administrator," Eastman said. "On occasion, she has served as a watchdog."

"She just happened to be working for the suspect contractors?" Gail shook her head. "Try again, gentlemen. That's too much of a coincidence."

Brady smiled—grimly, Gail thought.

"You're Monica's sister, all right," he told her. "Neither of you misses a trick. The fact is, as you know, it's fairly easy to pull strings to get an individual hired by a government contractor. In Monica's case, the employer gets a top-notch team player, and the government gets a very discreet alarm system."

"A spy." Gail said the word again under her breath, clasping her hands to still the trembling.

"And a good one," Eastman said after a pause. "Is that a problem for you?"

Gail rolled it around in her mind and finally shrugged. "I'm not sure, Mr. Eastman. I suppose it depends on what all this has to do with me—apart from the fact that Monica is my sister."

"We need your help, Ms. Montgomery," Brady told her, pressing his hands together. "Are you acquainted with Dr. Alex Shepard?"

"Of Vince Aircraft Company in Irving, Texas?" Gail replied, puzzled by the switch in subject matter. "Of course. He's considered to be America's leading aeronautical engineer." She had recently read a fascinating article on Shepard in *Science Digest*. "I know of him, but we've never met."

"You are familiar with Monarch Space Center in Tullahoma, Tennessee?" Brady asked.

Gail nodded. The wind tunnels at Monarch were used by aerospace engineers to test wind stress on advanced aircraft designs. Her own experiments were conducted in wind tunnels nearer to Martindale's research facility.

"Shepard and his colleague, Dr. Tom Armstrong, are staging top-secret tests at Monarch," Brady said. "How would you like to join them?"

Gail felt a nudge of excitement. Working with *the* Alex Shepard had long been one of her private fantasies. She couldn't believe that the possibility was now being dangled before her.

"When?" she asked.

"Immediately," Brady said. "As soon as you can be adequately briefed. Three days from now, at the absolute latest."

Gail sagged in her chair. "Impossible," she said, not even trying to conceal her disappointment. "I couldn't possibly get a leave of absence from my work here. Not right now."

Brady raised a hand, cutting off her protest. "That's already been taken care of. Dr. Calcutt is already making arrangements."

That news caught Gail completely off guard. As if to keep her off balance, Brady quickly continued.

"You'll be gone no more than two weeks—if you choose to accept," he said. "The final wind-tunnel tests are scheduled for early next week. Once those are successfully completed, you will be free to return to Martindale."

Gail sat motionless, still shaken to learn that Calcutt was prepared to find a stand-in for her on such short notice. Was she that easy to replace?

She looked first at Brady and then at Eastman. "All right, gentlemen, you have my attention," she conceded. "But I'm not about to go traipsing off to Tennessee for two weeks unless you give me more reason than you have so far. Not for Shepard—or anyone else. And need I remind you that we were discussing my sister, before you so neatly diverted my attention?"

"Give me time, Ms. Montgomery," Brady said. "We'll cover all bases." He seemed to relax, apparently satisfied that her decision was now a foregone conclusion. "I'll keep this as simple as I possibly can, because quite frankly, that's the only way *I* understand it," he went on. "Forgive me if this sounds like a kindergarten primer. I don't pretend to be a scientist.

"Shepard and Armstrong are only days away from final wind-tunnel tests on an advanced pilotless drone aircraft, code-named Shadow."

Gail leaned forward, her gaze suddenly riveted on the NSA agent. "Shadow? Is this drone something like the Stealth bomber? Can it avoid detection by radar?"

Brady's mouth dropped open, and Eastman started as if he had received a shock. "How did you know?" Brady asked.

"Dr. Shepard's experiments in Stealth technology are common knowledge," Gail explained, trying to curb her impatience. "The code name—Shadow—is a dead giveaway."

When Brady looked profoundly impressed by her powers of deduction, Gail decided that he wasn't being unduly modest about his rudimentary grasp of the subject.

"This is not a Stealth project," Brady said, clearing his throat and plowing on. "Shadow is an unarmed drone equipped solely for intelligence-gathering purposes. It is controlled by an extremely sophisticated on-board computer system—highly experimental at this stage—that can analyze incoming data while the drone is still over a target area.

"The aircraft is not controlled from the ground. The preprogrammed computer is in command at all times. Shadow flies itself to the target—gathers intelligence data itself with a variety of photographic and sensor equipment—orders the data transmission via satellite back to its base station—and if the on-board analysis system detects a threat of any kind, Shadow can even order its own self-destruction."

Brady squinted at his hands and licked his lips. Gail could tell he was straining to recall additional features of the drone in an effort to impress her. Hoping to learn more, she refrained from telling him that she was already fascinated.

"I guess you could say that Shadow has a mind of its own," Brady went on. "It's much more than just a spy in the sky. It represents a major breakthrough in obtaining the very latest intelligence information in trouble spots around the world."

"I thought spy satellites already did that," Gail said.

"Not at Shadow's close range," he said. "Shadow could fly over Baghdad and tell us what's on Saddam Hussein's breakfast table."

Gail couldn't help smiling at his undoubtedly exaggerated assessment of the drone's capabilities. "But what does all this have to do with me or with Monica?" she asked.

"For the past eight months, your sister has been working with Dr. Shepard as Shadow's assistant project manager." Brady waited for Gail to recover from that statement, then added, "And we have reason to believe she was about to sound a loud alarm."

Gail swallowed dryly, her mind reeling. Instead of clarifying the picture for her, Brady's explanation seemed to be growing more and more fantastic. Again she found herself almost wanting to disbelieve him. And again her eyes were drawn to the picture of Monica—to the phantomlike sibling whom she could no more deny now than she could turn her back on her own existence.

"Why?" Gail had to strain to get the word out.

"The Shadow project is vital to the country's intelligence-gathering community," Eastman put in, his sonorous voice edged with urgency. "The development team is made up of the cream of our aeronautical scientists. Monica entered the picture when it became apparent that there was a Brutus on the team."

"A what?" Gail automatically turned to Brady for a translation.

"Brutus slew Caesar," Brady said, raising an eyebrow at Eastman. "A leak of Shadow's technology could effectively kill the project, and set back national defense technology by ten years or more. Monica was our plumber, so to speak—until she vanished this week."

"Then her disappearance is related to Shadow?"

Brady shrugged and spread his hands. "That seems highly likely. She was to meet with me at a prearranged location two days ago. She never showed up."

Gail's roller-coasting emotions took another nosedive. "Has she been *harmed?*" she asked, filled with dread.

Eastman spread his hands. "Possibly. We certainly hope not. I can assure you, we are doing everything within our power to find her."

Brady took a deep breath, as if preparing to attempt one final and difficult hurdle. "Ms. Montgomery, your sister's absence leaves us in a difficult position," he said. "We've managed to temporarily cover for her. But in order to keep her previous efforts from going to waste, we need someone to replace Monica during Shadow's final tests next week. Someone to *be* Monica. For obvious reasons, that someone is you."

A long half minute passed before what he was asking of her fully registered. Even then, she couldn't quite believe Brady was serious.

"You want me to *impersonate* a sister I've never met? Be a member of a research team that I've never set eyes on? During critical final tests on a complex project that I know next to nothing about?" Gail sat back in her chair and laughed humorlessly. "You're out of your minds!"

"The plan isn't so ill-conceived as it sounds," Brady resumed. "Monica has maintained a detailed file on her work, which we've organized into a sort of game book of Shadow and the team. You'll be thoroughly briefed, so you won't be going in blind. We're confident you can handle the assignment. After all, you've had previous acting experience."

"Have I, indeed?" Gail said sardonically. "Please refresh my memory."

"In high school," Brady told her. "You starred in *The King and I* and *Pygmalion*."

"High school." Gail looked briefly at the ceiling, gamely resisting an urge to laugh hysterically. "Since your security check has obviously been painstakingly thorough, you surely know that I bombed both times."

The two men looked startled. "You got raves in the class yearbook," Brady pointed out.

"I was practically engaged to the yearbook editor that winter." It gave Gail a perverse sense of pleasure to burst their bubble. She did not appreciate being manipulated. "In all honesty, gentlemen, I can't act my way out of a paper bag. World's worst liar."

Eastman looked as if he had just swallowed a large dose of foul-tasting medicine. Brady merely winced and said reassuringly, "You'll do fine. You're so much like Monica in looks and personality, you won't need to act much. Of course, you will need to be careful."

"I don't recall agreeing to do this," Gail told the two men, although she had already made up her mind. Monica and the risk of danger aside, the allure of working with the great Alex Shepard was simply too seductive to resist. She couldn't help but gain from the experience, even over so short a period.

"You will be doing your country a great service, Ms. Montgomery," Eastman said. Clad in his civilian pinstripes, the Defense Intelligence officer seemed decidedly unmilitary, something which instilled in her a certain amount of confidence that their bizarre scheme might just work.

"I can't get over the fact that my twin, whom I didn't know existed, just happens to be involved in the same kind of work as I am," Gail observed. "It seems like another of those too-large-to-swallow coincidences."

"As assistant project manager, Monica was not directly involved in the technology itself," Eastman said smoothly. "She served more as a liaison between the chief engineer, Shepard, and Shadow's project test manager, Dr. Armstrong. Monica underwent an intensive crash course on the project before she stepped in. And she proved to be remarkably resourceful—as I'm sure you will, Ms. Montgomery."

"Are Monica and I resourceful—or just incredibly convenient?" Gail asked, anger making her voice tight.

As far as she was concerned, their lengthy silence confirmed her suspicion. Gail resented having been penciled in as a fail-safe backup for Monica without being told beforehand and wondered what Monica would think of the arrangement.

Gail chewed the corner of her lower lip, while both men watched her. Then she took the plunge, feeling her pulse shift into high gear even as she nodded.

"All right—when do we begin?" she asked, with a giddy sense that she was plummeting downhill on a runaway roller coaster.

Brady's smile became expansive. "This evening," he replied. "And believe me, Ms. Montgomery, you will not regret this."

Minutes later Gail wasn't so sure. She followed them out and when they were gone, closed the door and leaned against it, still filled with mixture of confusion, apprehension and excitement. *Monica. Alex Shepard.*

The palms of her hands grew clammy and her mind did wild gymnastics, vaulting ahead into the unknown.

The flashbacks kept coming—chilling visions of a tiny image of herself. Gail returned to her desk to study the snapshot of her flesh-and-blood look-alike,

Monica Seabury. The reality was almost too huge to grasp.

For that matter, so was the charade in which Gail had agreed to participate at Monarch Space Center. Now that it was too late to back out, she wondered what in God's name she had gotten herself into.

GAIL CALLED ALICIA to inform her that she would be going out of town for a week or so. She was relieved to hear Alicia's answering machine, recorded a quick message and hung up. Brady and Eastman might be convinced that she would be able to pull the wool over the eyes of Monica's co-workers at the Monarch Space Center. But Gail knew from experience that she could never fabricate an alibi that would satisfy Alicia.

Moments later, Gail entered Dr. Calcutt's office. He stepped around his desk and reached for her hands. "I'm having second thoughts, Gail," he said, frowning, resting his hazel eyes kindly upon her.

"Join the club." Gail laughed dryly. She studied his weathered, wrinkled face and felt warmth flow over her, realizing just how fond she had grown of this fatherly man during her years at Martindale.

"It's never too late to change your mind," Calcutt said.

Gail shook her head. "I've already given my word. And you taught me never to be a quitter."

He chuckled. "Gail, my dear, I suspect that you haven't been a quitter since the day you were born."

Since the day Monica and I were born, Gail wanted to say. But she caught herself. Calcutt hadn't been told why she was leaving, other than that it was a matter of national security. She felt as if she were deceiving him by holding back. But Dr. Calcutt had dealt with top-secret government contracts at Martindale for decades. She knew he would be appalled if she even considered leaking information to him.

He released her hands. "I have a feeling you are about to embark on a tremendous adventure, Gail."

"You might say that." Gail thought he had just made the understatement of the century. "But I still don't think it's fair to leave you in the lurch like this."

"Put that out of your mind," Calcutt told her firmly. "You have your propulsion project tightly organized. We can manage for the two weeks you'll be gone."

Gail tried to smile, and was jolted by the recognition that she was already thinking of Dr. Calcutt and Martindale Aircraft as elements of her past. She sensed that two weeks from now she would be different. Just knowing that Monica was out there somewhere had already made her different.

Monica. Monarch. Shadow. Alex Shepard. Gail wondered what else lay just over the horizon.

CHAPTER TWO

LATE-AFTERNOON SUNLIGHT angled through the trees as Gail pulled Monica's Porsche onto the highway shoulder behind a battered pickup truck. A gaunt man in greasy overalls rose from beside the jacked-up right rear wheel of the truck, a lug wrench in his fist, and squinted at her uncertainly. When she began unfolding a North Carolina highway map across the Porsche's leather-wrapped steering wheel, he glanced hesitantly toward the truck cab, then started toward her.

"Excuse me," Gail said as he bent at her window. "I'm a little confused by this map."

"Where you heading?" the man asked gruffly.

Gail looked up at him, surprised. She hadn't expected to run across a Yankee accent in the Great Smoky Mountains. He had one crooked eye that disturbed her, too, so she returned her attention to the map.

"To Pinehaven Retreat," she said. "It's a cabin located somewhere in this area—I hope."

The man abruptly backed away from the window and straightened. When Gail could no longer see his face, she couldn't help noticing his hands. They didn't seem grimy enough to go with the frayed overalls. On a second look, they appeared to have been recently manicured.

"Keep going about two more miles," he mumbled. "It's a big gate on the left. Can't miss it."

He ambled back to the truck before Gail could thank him. She shrugged, shifted the Porsche back into gear, and pulled back onto the highway.

As she accelerated past the pickup, she glanced into the cab, catching a fleeting glimpse of a bearded man in a dark slouch hat hunched down in the passenger seat. For some reason, her foot slipped over to the brake as she did a belated double take.

Gail frowned, wondering what had caused the reaction, and sped on down the highway. The day was growing short. If she didn't find Pinehaven before dark, she might be roaming around the unfamiliar countryside half the night.

She was still anxious and annoyed at having Pinehaven sprung upon her at the last moment. She had counted on dealing with the Shadow team only at the Monarch labs, where she would have felt some degree of familiarity. The sudden shift to Alex Shepard's secluded mountain retreat had thrown her for a loop.

Over and over again, Gail replayed the upcoming encounter in her mind. It turned out the same each time. With phony bravado, she strolled right up to the towering scientist—in her awestruck imagination Alex Shepard towered even more than he did in reality. He slowly looked her up and down with a deeply pene- trating gaze that sent a devastating tremor through her deception as if it were a geological fault. He didn't say anything. He didn't have to. He simply stood there shaking his head, close enough to touch, but forever beyond her reach.

That was hardly the scenario that Dick Brady and Howard Eastman had in mind. The agents had been thorough in preparing Gail for her debut, right down to appropriating Monica's clothes and car. The car in particular bothered her.

When he had handed Gail the keys at the Asheville airport that afternoon, Brady had mentioned that they had picked up the car at Monica's Tullahoma, Tennessee apartment complex. Knowing that Mon- ica had disappeared without her car forced Gail to fi- nally accept the strong likelihood that her sister had dropped out of sight against her will. The thought that Monica might have met some unspeakably hor- rible end—that they might never have a chance to know each other—sickened Gail.

She forced herself to concentrate on steering the Porsche along the winding, deserted highway, watching tensely for the gate to Pinehaven. The closer she got, the less confident she was that she would remember even a fraction of the contents of the three-inch-thick loose-leaf notebook that was her script for the Shadow game.

Less than half a mile from the spot where she'd encountered the pickup truck, Gail spotted a crudely painted sign nailed to a tree to the left of the highway, alongside what appeared to be a rough logging road. Pinehaven. She braked sharply, twisted the steering wheel, and the exhilaratingly responsive sports car shot across the highway and into the mouth of the opening.

"Some big gate," she muttered in disgust, shifting down as the car began to climb.

The road quickly narrowed, degenerating into little more than a grassy trail. Gail kept going, the Porsche's engine grumbling throatily through stands of tall chestnut trees touched with fall colors. Now and then she spotted the French Broad River wending its way below.

The deep reds and yellows of the maples and sweet gums, mingling with towering evergreen pines, drove some of her apprehension away. Gail was even beginning to enjoy the scenery along Pinehaven's ridiculously primitive driveway, when the Porsche suddenly lurched to a halt, whipping her sharply against the shoulder harness.

"Damn!" Gail slapped the steering wheel hard with the flat of her hand. She tried shifting into Reverse and heard the wheels spin wildly. While ogling the scenery, she had gotten the low-slung car stuck on the rutted, uneven path.

"You'd have to be a goat to use this driveway," she muttered, running a hand through her hair, angry at her own stupidity.

In the game book, Monica hadn't mentioned the Pinehaven road being so bad. At least Gail didn't remember it. But then, perhaps she had been too caught up in reading the narrative to notice such a minor detail.

Reading Monica's words had been like poring over a report that Gail might have written herself. The phrasing—the *voice*—had been so similar to her own that it had actually given her chills.

Besides details related to her work, Monica had given her personal impressions of Pinehaven as well as of the Monarch research facility in Tennessee and the Shadow team. But there had been . . . *holes?* In a few places, particularly where Alex Shepard and Tom Armstrong were mentioned, there had been odd changes in the *voice*—almost as if those parts had been written by someone else.

If only she could have talked to Monica in person. Once again, Gail was aware of those almost-forgotten childhood memories of her other self. The emotions building within her now, however, were tempered with fear. A shudder passed through her body, and she wondered if her sister was even still alive.

With dusk closing in, there was already a decided chill in the mountain air. Gail felt disoriented, and had to remind herself that this was the way it would be for the foreseeable future. Glancing into the rearview mirror at her new short haircut, trimmed to match Monica's, only added to the unreality.

Grabbing Monica's suede jacket, she opened the car door and slid from behind the steering wheel. She slipped the jacket on. Like everything else that had been borrowed from Monica's apartment in Tullahoma, the garment was a perfect fit. Although she found that somehow reassuring, Gail was jarred by the touchable evidence of her twin's existence.

She knelt and peered beneath the Porsche at the high ridge of earth on which the sports car was firmly lodged. A trickle of oil snaked slowly along the grassy rut from the Porsche's punctured oil pan.

"Damn!" she said again. "What now?"

Gail walked away a few paces and sank onto a fallen log, momentarily defeated. She shivered at the thought of spending a cold night alone in Monica's car.

A distant sound cracked through the silence, startling her. Gail rose, turning her head to listen.

Woodcutters? The sound had not been loud, but it made her feel less alone in the forest.

She listened to the rhythmic chopping sound for a moment, then started walking in that direction, hoping the woodcutter wouldn't knock off for the day before she located him. Underbrush caught at her skirt, snagging her hose and slowing her progress.

The sounds seemed to grow fainter and farther apart. Suddenly desperate, Gail cried out, her voice ringing hollowly off the grove of tall conifers ahead. She made out a clearing just beyond the clump of firs, and stumbled toward it.

"Oh, Lord!" The cry choked in her throat as she stepped into the clearing and froze.

A man lay sprawled on his back, eyes closed, his face turned toward the cloudless sky. Panic welled momentarily; Gail saw a rivulet of blood oozing from an ugly gash at his temple. At first she thought he must be dead, he lay so utterly still. Then he groaned, and his thick chest swelled beneath his plaid wool shirt.

Gail crossed the small clearing and knelt at his side. "Can you hear me?" She spoke softly and got no response.

She couldn't determine the depth of the wound. She fumbled in her jacket pockets for a handkerchief—anything to stanch the sickening flow of blood. Her fingers closed around a scrap of paper.

Gail pulled it out, hurriedly glancing at it just long enough to determine that it was some sort of hand-written note. Perhaps something that Monica had written? Mentally handcuffed by a sudden rush of emotion, she stared at it.

The man groaned again, snapping Gail back to a sense of urgency. Here she was alone in the woods with an injured man, and she didn't have so much as a Kleenex. She felt totally helpless.

Gail glanced around, noting the double-bitted ax lying just beyond his fingertips and the newly felled tree near his body. The cause of the accident seemed obvious. Yet there was something about the angles of ax, man and tree that didn't seem quite right.

Pressing her fingers against his neck, Gail detected a strong pulse. Relieved, she fingered a thick wave of tawny hair from his broad forehead, tracing the line of his slightly receding hairline to the very edge of the gash—and sucked in her breath.

Shepard! Her hand jerked away from his face—the same face she had studied so carefully in the person-nel section of Monica's Shadow game book. Unlike the stern intensity depicted in the photo, Alex Shep-ard's face in repose looked vulnerable and much younger than his thirty-seven years. Still, it was a strong, virile-looking face.

He murmured something, his eyelids fluttering. Gail leaned closer to hear. "What?" she asked.

Before she realized what was happening, his muscular arm arched up around her neck. "Darling," he murmured, pulling her down until their lips crushed together. Her mind went blank, and a tingle of bewildering pleasure made her gasp. Then his arm went limp once again, and he released her with a sigh.

Gail sat back on her heels, shaking her head to clear her mind. Her breathing quavered. For an instant she wondered if he had really kissed her. She touched his cheek tentatively, feeling the stubble of his whiskers against her fingers, and he moaned again.

"Oh, God," she breathed, "how badly are you hurt?"

Her lips burned, as if in reply to her question. Gail swallowed hard. How badly *could* he be hurt and still kiss like that? Without even fully regaining consciousness!

Jumping to her feet, Gail frantically searched the edge of the clearing for a path—a clue—*anything* that might steer her steps in the right direction. From what sounded like only a short distance away, the sharp ring of another ax echoed through the wood.

"Thank you, God," she said under her breath. "Thank you, thank you, thank you."

With an anxious parting look at Alex Shepard lying motionless in the grass, Gail took off at a run toward the sound of the chopping—just as it stopped.

Springing, stumbling over the rugged ground, Gail opened her mouth and shouted at the top of her lungs. "Help!" A dozen paces farther, she repeated the cry.

A young man holding an ax suddenly appeared on the next ridge, crashing toward her through the underbrush. She just had time to register that he was in his early teens, but large for his age, before he reached her.

"Help me!" she gasped, out of breath. "Dr. Shepard is down here, hurt!"

She motioned back toward the clearing. The young man dropped his ax and stampeded past her toward the clearing without breaking stride. Gail turned and followed, barely managing to keep up.

"Alex!" The boy raced into the clearing, his voice shrill with panic, and skidded to his knees at the fallen engineer's side. "What happened?"

He looked up at Gail, his black eyes stricken. Then, leaning over, he placed his ear to the man's chest. "He's still breathing."

Definitely, Gail thought, her fingers going to her lips.

"I'm all right, Rafe," Alex whispered hoarsely without opening his eyes, stirring slightly.

Gail dropped beside the young man, grateful to be able to attach a name to the youth, since the contents of the game book had temporarily flown from her memory. Had Monica even mentioned a Rafe?

Alex opened his eyes slowly. Half-conscious, at best, he appeared to be straining to focus on her face. "Monica?"

Gail gave a start at hearing the name directed at her for the first time. The drama had begun. Her first hurdle had even been conquered, she realized, although not in the way it had been planned. She had made an unscripted entrance onto the unfamiliar stage.

"Is he hurt bad?" Rafe asked anxiously, his face contorted with concern.

"I don't know, Rafe," she said, trying to remain calm. "But we have to find a way to get him to the cabin. He needs a doctor."

"I can walk," Alex rasped, his words slurred.

"Sure you can," Gail retorted. "We'll all hold hands and skip down the yellow brick road, like in *The Wizard of Oz.*"

Alex closed one eye and peered at her. She wondered if he was seeing double, or if she was beginning to sound as crazy as she felt. Gail clenched her fists and told herself to shape up. If she couldn't even fool a man in the throes of a brain concussion, she might as well give up and go home.

"Rafe, help me up," Alex said, flopping an arm across the boy's chest.

Rafe looked questioningly at Gail, obviously torn between obeying orders and following common sense. Gail shook her head.

"Uh, Alex," Rafe said, "maybe you ought to just sit tight for a spell. I'll hightail it back home and get my pa to bring his truck up."

"Don't be an old woman about this, Rafe." Alex clawed a handful of Rafe's shirt and pulled himself to a sitting position. He grimaced, holding his head with his free hand. For a moment he looked as if he would throw up. "Damned tree."

"You're going to kill your fool self if you don't lie back down," Gail said.

Alex grinned or grimaced again—she couldn't tell which. Gail had a horrible vision of him succumbing to a blood clot on the brain right then and there. With an almost physical stab of guilt, she wondered if she was more concerned with his health or with preserving her own opportunity to work with him. She fingered her lips, bewildered by emotions that seemed to come at her from all directions.

Rafe seemed to give up talking him out of moving, and tucked his narrow shoulder under Alex's arm. While Gail watched helplessly, the two counted in unison, and came to their feet on three with a roar that seemed to fill the clearing. Alex tottered drunkenly, and she was sure he would crash down like the very tree that had apparently felled him. But Rafe managed to get him braced.

Gail rose beside Alex, amazed at how much larger he was than he had looked on the ground. Wide shoulders tapered to a flat abdomen and trim hips. His legs seemed to go on forever, although they were wobbly at the knees at the moment.

"You know this is insane," she said grimly.

Alex squeezed his eyes shut, then opened them. He was definitely having vision problems. Gail reached up and pressed her fingertips to his neck just below his jaw to check his pulse again. He sucked in his breath and looked at her oddly.

"I'll tell you about insane," he said. "Before the roof caved in, I'd swear I heard some idiot trying to drive something with a high-performance engine up the old logging road."

Logging road. Gail's fingers curled into themselves. The turnoff hadn't been Pinehaven's driveway, after all. Alex was right: he had heard an idiot.

"That was me," she confessed. "I got stuck."

Rocking slightly, Alex stared at her with a look of intense concentration. "I don't believe I'm up to discussing that just now," he said finally.

He draped his right arm around Rafe's shoulder, and pulled Gail snugly under his left. Gail hesitated, then put an arm around his waist; he drew her close against his muscular body. They turned and started slowly up the ridge toward the cabin, her hand pressing against his heaving rib cage. She felt a tingle in her fingertips—a startlingly electrical sensation that moved in stages up her arm and into her body.

"Glad you're back, Monica," Alex said, shuffling along heavy-footedly between Gail and Rafe.

He squeezed her shoulder, sending another surge of tingling into Gail's body. She had never been so vividly aware of masculinity before. And it wasn't entirely due to the kiss, which she was coming to think of as some sort of weird reflex reaction on Alex's part.

You've never had a man lean on you like this, she thought. In an odd sort of way, his unsteady weakness made Alex seem all the more virile.

"It's gonna be a fun party tonight," Alex muttered glumly. "Damned tree."

"Are you sure the tree fell on you, Alex?" Rafe asked, helping him maneuver around a deadfall.

"*Something* did," Alex said. "Don't remember."

Gail looked past him at Rafe, meeting the boy's black eyes with a frown. "What are you getting at, Rafe?" she asked.

"Nothing," Rafe replied, with a scowl that looked too old for his years. "I just thought I heard someone running through the woods just before you hollered. Must have been a deer or something."

Or something. Gail glanced up at Alex's bunched face. He seemed to be concentrating on putting one foot in front of the other. She couldn't tell if he was thinking what she was thinking—that something or someone might have played a part in his injury.

The cabin was just over the next rise. Gail was impressed by Alex's iron will when he made it all the way without stopping to rest.

They slowly climbed the split-log steps to a wide veranda that ran along two sides of the dwelling. The place was a lot more imposing than Monica's rough sketch had led Gail to anticipate. They stepped through a wide doorway into an enormous living room furnished in warm earth tones. Ceiling-high bookcases flanked a six-foot-tall fireplace of unchiseled granite mortared together to look like a natural rock formation.

It was unlike any fireplace Gail had ever seen, and she could imagine Alex Shepard having a hand in the design of the massive structure. She moved into the room, finding herself smiling at its cozy cheerfulness. Above the mantle hung a large painting of a mountain sunrise with the initials *A.S.* scrawled in one corner, reminding Gail of Alex's reputation as an accomplished artist.

She would never have expected to find a retreat this elaborate, hidden so far off the beaten path. She suddenly felt that she was opening a door into the very heart of the man's character—the same man who was now stumbling toward the long couch with her help.

As they lowered Alex heavily to the cushions, Gail stole a look at the hand-hewn oak stairway leading to the cabin's second floor. There was no way that she and Rafe would be able to wrestle their patient up those stairs to his bedroom.

One glance at Alex's face in the lamplight increased Gail's concern for him. He was obviously still in pain, and she wanted to help him. But to do that, she had to overcome a sudden, inexplicable shyness about touching him.

"Head injury—head up," she murmured, scrounging the first-aid rule from some cobwebbed corner of her memory. Alex did not object as she squeezed a throw pillow under his head. Next, she took an afghan from one end of the couch and tucked it securely around him.

"There's so much blood!" she exclaimed.

"Damned tree blindsided me," Alex murmured, closing his eyes. "Lord, what a headache!"

"Don't you dare go to sleep, Alex," Gail said anxiously, fearful that if he did, he might never wake up again. But when she glanced up and saw Rafe's distraught expression, she forced herself to smile and say, "He'll be fine, Rafe."

Rafe didn't seem reassured. He rubbed both hands hard down his thighs, chewing on his lip. "What can I do?" he asked.

Gail realized that he was expecting her to get a grip on the situation. She had to get a grip on herself first. *What would Monica do?* Gail didn't have a clue. So she went with the first thing that popped into her mind—anything to help Rafe cope.

"Go boil some water," she said, winging it. "Let's see if we can get the wound cleaned up enough to see how bad it is. And while you're at it, Rafe, you'd better go ahead and call a doctor."

Alex growled a protest. "Just let me rest, for Pete's sake," he said irritably. "You call a doctor, and I'll pink-slip the lot of you."

Gail pursed her lips in exasperation. But Rafe seemed cheered by Alex's irascibility and left the living room with a grin on his face. He apparently had the good sense to not take Gail's instructions literally and returned moments later with a pan of warm water and a stack of kitchen towels.

"Should I make a fire?" Rafe asked Gail, placing the pan upon the floor next to the couch.

Before she could answer, Alex said, "Don't forget the damper this time, knothead."

Rafe's grin broadened. "Yes, *sir!*"

Gail massaged the spot between her eyes with the ball of her index finger, inching up on a headache of her own. Then, with Rafe busy at the stone hearth, she dipped a clean cloth into the pan of water and began gingerly sponging the blood from Alex's face.

As she leaned over him, she was tremulously aware of his warm breath on her face. Up close—closer than she had ever dreamed of being to the esteemed Dr. Alex Shepard—Gail found herself enthralled by his ruggedly handsome features. Even in his current condition, the strong contours of his face seemed stamped with intelligence. His hair, falling soft and shiny against his tanned forehead, released a spicy, musky fragrance.

"Sorry," she said as he winced. She soaked a fresh cloth and resumed dabbing at the wide ribbon of blood that had trailed down the side of his face to soak his shirt.

Alex's thick lashes fluttered open, and his dark gaze focused on her with obvious difficulty, a deep scowl grooving his forehead. Gail concentrated on mopping up the mess, relieved that the blood had clotted. Mindful of the pain she had inadvertently caused him a moment earlier, she approached the immediate area of the wound with extreme caution.

"I don't think the gash is as deep as I'd feared," she said. He lay perfectly still, his expression rigid, while she barely touched the edges of the wound with a fingertip. "Maybe you're just what's known as a healthy bleeder."

"I think it was more than one," he said, suddenly pensive.

"More than one what?" Gail asked.

"Tree. I figured maybe three or four must've snuck up on me when my back was turned."

Gail stared at him blank-faced, wondering if Alex had slipped over the edge into some kind of hallucination. Rafe snorted. She shot a glance at the boy and blinked. If grins were a disease, Rafe's would be classed as terminal.

"Trees can be damned devious," Alex muttered.

"Is that a fact?" Gail was beginning to get the picture. The virile hunk of engineering genius lying on the couch before her had an off-the-wall sense of humor. Indeed, from the obvious rise in Rafe's spirits, that seemed to be a reliable indicator of Alex Shepard's state of health.

"Yeah." Alex pawed a big hand down his face. "Like when you're hiking along with your thinking cap on, and a big old oak ootches over to one side while you aren't looking, so you'll walk smack into it."

Gail twisted her mouth hard to one side to kill a smile. "I must say, you deal with pain very well," she commented.

When she turned to collect the stained towels, his hand came down over hers, engulfing it in a calloused grasp; it was so gentle that her skin prickled. She prayed he wouldn't notice.

"Did I tell you I'm glad you're back?" he asked.

"Yes," Gail managed.

"Did you tell me why you left?" he asked.

Gail froze, her mind scrabbling for an out. Alex tried to rise onto one elbow. She pressed him back, aware from the way he resisted that his strength was slowly returning. And equally aware that something deep within her quivered in response to his burgeoning power.

"Don't be doing that," she scolded. "If you insist on moving around, I'm going to call a doctor, anyway."

"How?" Alex asked. "You know there's no phone up here. That's one luxury I do without."

Gail was dumbstruck by her gaffe, recalling too late that Monica's Shadow script had specifically mentioned the lack of telephones and television sets at Pinehaven. She would have to be more careful. Before she could recover her mental balance, Alex smiled wryly.

"Wherever you went, it turned you into a damned bossy female," he said, with a pronounced note of appreciation. The smile faltered almost imperceptibly. "I can see Tom's in for a surprise."

Gail felt the undercurrent in his gaze. It was like an invisible hand brushing her cheek—a look she didn't understand.

"Rafe, get me a gin and tonic, will you?" Alex requested, abruptly breaking the connection, as if trying to draw away from a thought.

"No, Rafe!" Gail shot to her feet, nearly spilling the pan of red-tinted water. "Not with a head injury."

"I've had a concussion before," Alex told her. "I'll take care of it the way *I* want to."

"Come off it, Alex. You just might have a fractured skull," she said, holding her ground, feeling her tension finally boil to the surface. "Now, where can I find bandages and antiseptic—preferably something that stings like fire? Maybe I'll burn some sense into that head of yours."

Their gazes locked for one long, breathless moment. Then Alex slowly settled back onto the cushions. "Upstairs bathroom," he said evenly. "The one off the room you and Adelaide always share."

Gail turned on her heel and stalked toward the oak staircase, mentally matching the name with memorized information from the game book. She dreaded her first meeting with Adelaide Barber, who headed the project's computer-science section.

According to Monica, Adelaide was a sharp, demanding, ambitious iron maiden. Because of the woman's expertise in computers, Gail guessed that her weekend roommate would also have a penetrating eye for detail. She was bound to see through Gail's mostly ad-libbed portrayal of Monica.

Gail shoved that problem aside for the moment to deal with a more immediate one. She hoped to high heaven that she could remember the diagram Monica had made of the cabin's second floor. She was just reaching for the banister newel when Alex called to her from the couch.

"Monica!"

She spun around. "What?"

His face twitched. After a long pause, he said quietly, "I really am glad you're back."

Gail suddenly felt bone tired. This wasn't the way she was supposed to have made her entry into the Shadow project. From the moment she had mistakenly turned off the highway onto the old logging road, the situation had been out of her control. When she turned now and started climbing the stairway, feeling Alex's dark gaze stroking her back, Gail had an uneasy feeling that the Shadow adventure was not the only element in her future that threatened to get out of hand.

At the top of the stairway, she turned left and marched down the dimly lighted hallway to the first door on the left. She entered the front bedroom

Monica had shared with Adelaide on previous visits
to Pinehaven and found herself checking the door for
a lock. For some reason she needed to know there was
one.

CHAPTER THREE

THROUGH A THROBBING, nauseating headache that cast a milky blur across his vision, Alex watched Monica slowly climb the stairway. She moved gracefully, head erect, her delightful turned-up nose in contrast with the almost perfect symmetry of her face.

She could be right about the fractured skull. At least that might explain the strangely sensual images that had spiraled through his mind as her fingers moved ever so tenderly along his face, dabbing with the wet towels.

Had he been hallucinating? Or had he actually sensed a new kind of vulnerability about her? When he had called out to her as she reached the foot of the staircase, Alex had been on the verge of telling Monica that *she* would be fine.

That made no sense at all. Monica Seabury was one of the most self-assured people he knew. That was precisely why he had never allowed himself to become attracted to her as a woman. He simply didn't have the self-confidence to deal with someone like

Monica, except as the unknowing model for the portrait of his dreams.

So what had changed? Why did he suddenly sense a doelike uncertainty about her that struck such a resounding chord with his own hidden self-doubt?

Alex rubbed his eyes, trying to clear his vision, but knowing that only time would do that. He had never understood women and accepted the fault as entirely his own. Years of intense absorption in his work, often to the point of obsession, hadn't exactly left him with a world of experience with the fair sex—in spite of an unearned reputation to the contrary within Vince Aircraft's rumor mill.

Monica, in particular, was an enigma that he could ill afford to become involved with. Especially with his best friend looming so hugely in the picture. Monica was Tom's reality. For Alex she was merely a lovely canvas, upon which he painted a dream almost too precious to contemplate.

The dream. Maybe that was all it would ever be. Maybe he would never be as fortunate as Tom, who wanted only to love a flesh-and-blood woman. But that was the price that Alex would pay for wanting something more—for wanting a soul mate.

"Dream on," Alex whispered under his breath.

"Say something?"

Alex looked up at Rafe, who was leaning over the back of the couch. The boy was a haystack of sharp adolescent angles. But when Rafe picked up one of Alex's fine sable-hair paint brushes, the kid put aside his coltish awkwardness and became an artist of remarkable raw talent.

Alex still could not believe how much he had come to love the boy, even to the point of wishing Rafe were his own son, though Rafe already had a family of his own: a father and five brothers and sisters on a dilapidated hardscrabble farm down the mountain. So Alex had to settle for being the boy's self-appointed godfather.

"Just the ravings of a delirious patient," Alex said, returning Rafe's guileless smirk. "You aren't going to get me that drink, are you?"

Rafe stabbed a meaningful look toward the staircase. "I don't think it's worth the risk."

Alex grunted. "Maybe you're right. Monica seems to have grown spurs while she was gone."

He curled his full lower lip over the upper, pondering that for a moment before casting the thought aside. He would probably wake up tomorrow minus the grinding headache and find that Monica was her same old self, after all.

"It's getting late," he said, shifting his attention back to Rafe. "You ought to be heading on home, kiddo."

Rafe nodded and settled himself onto the arm of the couch at Alex's feet. He looked pensive. "Don't you want me to hang around until everyone gets here?'' he asked.

"No need. The one-woman Gestapo seems to have everything under control.'' Alex pointed at the ceiling and Rafe laughed out loud.

The kid had a good laugh. With luck—and all the help Alex could provide without ruining him—that laugh and a fistful of sable-hair paintbrushes would carry Rafe far.

The laugh died away, followed by the smile. Alex could tell something was eating at the boy, but the way his own head was splitting open, he didn't want to have to deal with a fourteen-year-old's problems right then. All the same, buried way down deep where he hardly ever got a look at it, Alex still had enough of a boy in him to understand how monumentally difficult it was for a kid of Rafe's age to sit on a thought for any length of time at all.

"Spit it out, brat,'' Alex said, hoping Rafe didn't hit him with anything radical.

"Alex, you taught me to be very careful with an ax,'' Rafe observed, knitting his bony fingers together.

"Uh-huh. So leave it to me to be the one who messed up.''

"Did you?'' Rafe looked hard at him, as if willing Alex to see his thoughts. "Did you really get blindsided by a tree? You were chopping away at it, and you didn't know it was getting close—that it was about to come down?''

"You want the honest truth, Rafe?"

The boy nodded.

"I have no idea," Alex admitted. "I don't remember anything between when I took the first few whacks at the tree, and when you leaned over me out there in the clearing."

That wasn't entirely true. He'd had a vague impression of being touched by cool, gentle fingers. And his lips—he remembered something like warm, heady wine against his lips. Had all that been only a dream?

"Now that I think about it," Rafe said, frowning, "I don't think that was a deer I heard running through the woods."

"Running. What direction?"

"Away. Toward the highway, as best I could tell," Rafe said. "I didn't get a look at it, but it sounded like a two-legged animal to me."

Alex turned that over in his mind and sighed. He knew very well what Rafe was getting at, but it didn't make sense. Nobody would go to that much trouble to assault a woodcutter that far off the beaten path. He hadn't even been carrying a wallet.

Besides, only a handful of people even knew he was at Pinehaven this weekend. Rafe. Half a dozen members of the Shadow project team. No—he could see no point in following that track.

"Rafe, if you're going to play detective, you'll have to learn the theory of motivation," he said, putting on a crooked smile solely for the boy's benefit. "The only person who would possibly have wanted to hurt me was that tree. I was killing it."

Rafe's jaw slid to one side as he thought about it. Then he grinned. "A tree isn't a person."

"That depends on your religion, my boy," Alex said, closing his eyes. "Now scat. I have company coming, and I need to rest up for some wanton debauchery."

"Oh, wow! Another Friday night with the wild bunch!" Rafe exclaimed, and slid off the arm of the couch. "See you tomorrow."

A moment later, Alex heard the front door close. Softly. Rafe was very considerate. Alex drew an arm across his eyes, shutting out the dim lamplight. But he couldn't shut down his thoughts. They stomped around inside his throbbing head, giving him no peace.

Why had Monica suddenly taken off, right in the middle of Shadow's final test? She had left a written request for an emergency leave of absence on his desk, which he had only found after she had gone. Like some kind of dippy military procedure, he thought. Her surprise move had left even Tom in the dark.

Or so Tom claimed. Suspecting that a glitch had occurred in Tom's relationship with Monica, Alex had avoided riding the situation too hard. For now he would just be grateful to have her back on the team. He was prepared to wait and see if a reasonable explanation surfaced without having to demand one.

The questions just kept piling up, though. What on earth was Monica doing driving her Porsche up that old logging trail? And why couldn't he remember a tree falling right on top of him?

GAIL REACHED into the medicine cabinet and grabbed a roll of gauze. As she crammed it into her jacket pocket, she felt a wad of crumpled paper. Remembering the note that she had discovered earlier, she pulled it out and unfolded it. The neat script was eerily similar to her own. It had to be Monica's handwriting.

Sister—
    Mountain Park Motel, #209. Saturday, 10:00 a.m.
    Caution!
    M.

Stunned, Gail sagged against the door frame. For a long moment she couldn't get her breath as she read and reread the note. For the first time she held the reality of Monica in her hands. Trembling, she crushed the slip of paper to her breast and closed her eyes. Monica was alive!

"Come on, Gail, pull yourself together," she murmured. "You have work to do."

She wondered fleetingly how Monica knew that she would find the note. But that was just one more item to add to her growing list of unanswered questions. For now, Gail had her work cut out for her.

Glancing into the lavatory mirror, she frowned. She was a mess, almost as pale and drawn as her patient downstairs.

Streaks of Alex's blood spotted her cheek where she had wiped the back of her hand. Her legs were scratched and bleeding, her hose in a hundred runs. Even her arms and shoulders ached from bearing part of his weight as Alex had staggered up to the cabin from the clearing.

Seventy-two hours earlier, she had been sitting down to a microwaved supper in her colorless apartment on the other side of the continent. Now she felt as if she was flailing around in treacherous waters, far out of her depth.

Gail shook off the thought and stepped out of the tiled bathroom. She crossed the carpeted guest bedroom and had already stepped into the upstairs hallway when she stopped and looked back into the room in which she would probably spend the night with Adelaide Barber.

Her gaze shifted back and forth between the twin beds. There were a thousand details that nobody had thought to include in the Shadow game book, any one of which might give her away. Gail considered one of them now. Which of the twin beds had Monica slept in on previous visits to Pinehaven?

She closed the door on the thought, started back down the hallway toward the staircase and stopped again. She could hear Rafe talking quietly with Alex downstairs. This might be her only opportunity to familiarize herself with the upstairs beyond the rudimentary layout of Monica's diagram.

Backtracking quickly, she peeked into an open doorway to the right. A small light burned in an overhead fixture, providing just enough illumination to make out the sparse furnishings of a studio. Easels. Canvases stacked against the walls. A large drawing board. She glanced up at a huge skylight. The Shadow script had mentioned that Alex painted as a hobby, but this studio indicated a much deeper interest than that.

Gail was intrigued by the glimpse of the man behind the scientist, but there wasn't time to go on in. If she snooped too long, she would be missed downstairs. Reluctantly she moved on.

The next door opened into another bedroom. Twin beds again. Gail had no idea who ordinarily occupied the room. She dodged down to the end of the hallway and tried one more door. One double bed this time. That did present some interesting possibilities.

If memory served her correctly, besides Adelaide, three more guests had yet to arrive at Pinehaven. Tom Armstrong, Shadow's project test manager, who was also Alex's longtime friend and colleague back at Vince Aircraft in Texas. Dorie Pryor, Adelaide's assistant engineering project manager in Shadow's computer section. And Joe Anderson, the computer software salesman whom Dorie had met in Brevard. How the trio chose to divide the two remaining guest rooms, Gail decided, might be revealing, if not downright titillating.

One more door. Gail crept across the hallway and opened it. This bedroom obviously belonged to the master of Pinehaven. She could not resist turning on the light. Muted track lighting cast a soft glow over the huge bed, a hulking dresser against one wall, and more than a little bachelor clutter.

She had a sense that this was Alex's very private lair. For some reason, her eyes were drawn as if by magnets to the bed. Only belatedly did she notice a large, cloth-draped easel near the expansive window across the back wall. She had already drifted halfway toward it before she realized she had actually entered the room.

Gail stopped at the easel, lifted the cloth drape— and stood stunned. She stared wide-eyed at what appeared to be a portrait of herself. There was something faintly seductive about the image, but it was more than that. It was as if someone had painted her soul.

She let the drapery fall back into place, still feeling dazed. But her natural curiosity demanded a second look. As she stared at her likeness once again, a strange sensation swept over her.

Monica! For a moment she had completely forgotten about her sister. Of course, this was Monica's portrait, not her own. Monica captured on canvas, so vibrant, seductively lovely, with an invitation in her gray-blue eyes.

Gail's throat went dry. Gazing transfixed at the painting, she felt her heart plummet inexplicably into despair. She sensed more than Monica in the portrait. There in the bold brush strokes, as well as in the delicately feathered detail, she could almost *feel* the artist's emotions.

Had Monica actually posed for the portrait? Gail studied the dreamlike quality of the painting, wondering. When she tried to imagine Alex standing at the easel, baring his own soul as he applied layer upon layer of oil paint to the canvas, Gail couldn't bear to look at it any longer.

She hurried from the room and passed the guest-room doors again, wondering distractedly if one of the beds might hold a Brutus that night. Of course,

Howard Eastman had been referring to a potential murderer of the Shadow project—not of a human being—when he had used the term. But in the light of Alex's lucky escape in the clearing this afternoon, the thought made her shudder.

At the head of the stairway Gail took a deep breath, trying to calm herself. With or without a Brutus in the house, she could not erase the erotic portrait from her mind. The confusing insight into Alex's character excited her, even as it filled her with a strange kind of foreboding.

Halfway down to the living room, she caught a snatch of conversation between Alex and Rafe— "I have company coming..."—and almost tripped. For a moment she couldn't take another step. By the time she realized that she was being gripped by pure stage fright, Rafe had come into view. The boy moved lankily past the foot of the staircase and let himself out the front door.

Gail tightened her fist on the banister. So far she had fooled Alex—with the help of his concussion. But there was nothing jangled about Rafe's senses, and the boy had given no indication that he suspected anything was amiss with Monica. Gail told herself that if she could just make it through the next twenty-four hours, she just might be able to bring off this whole charade. She lifted her chin and marched on down the stairs.

ALEX SENSED, rather than heard, Monica enter the living room. Ever since regaining consciousness in the clearing, he seemed to be operating on an incredibly elevated sensory level where she was concerned.

He drew his arm away from his face and looked up at her through the haze. She stood before him like a photograph taken with a soft-focus lens. *Like an image in a dream.*

"You really do look ghastly," the image said.

The dream crashed against reality at the sound of her voice. The truth was, he felt pretty ghastly. Worse still, he knew that how he felt wasn't entirely due to the blow he had taken on the head. If he didn't get his mind off Monica and back where it belonged—on Shadow—the blasted headache was going to be the least of his worries.

"Lie still while I see what I can do with a little Merthiolate and tape," Monica said, kneeling beside the couch. She unloaded her jacket pockets, spreading her first-aid supplies upon his chest.

"How does it happen you're such a good nurse?" Alex asked, his eyes watering as she carefully swabbed on the antiseptic.

"I'm not. It just seems that way in contrast, because you're being such a terrible patient," she said, deftly applying a gauze dressing to his temple. "You really should see a doctor."

"I *am* a doctor," he said.

"Remind me of that the next time I get a strep infection, *Dr.* Shepard. I'm sure you'll come in real handy."

There was tension in her voice. But Alex barely felt the strips of papery surgical tape being smoothed into place. The gossamer lightness of her touch sent a startling vibration down the length of his body. Alex sat up too fast, dumping the tape spool and Merthiolate bottle off his chest, and making his head swim.

Damn! What was getting into him? Had the concussion jangled his brain to the point where he could no longer control his own thoughts and emotions? The very idea of what he was feeling toward Monica Seabury—*Tom's Monica*—rocked him with guilt.

He pawed his shirt pockets, producing the small notebook and pencil stub that he always carried for those odd moments when he might be struck by an inspiration—instead of by a tree. He had to keep his mind occupied with less hazardous subject matter until he regained his good sense.

"Alex, stay down!" Monica protested.

"Monica, *sit* down," he ordered, jabbing a finger at the couch cushion next to him.

She hung back, and Alex regretted having spoken so sharply. Then she slid onto the cushion. He opened the notebook and discovered at once that squinting at it made his head hurt worse. He gritted his teeth and began sketching, forcing his thoughts into submission to his brute will.

"Look here," he said, roughing out the familiar lines of the Shadow drone with quick, hard strokes of the pencil. "While you were gone, I came up with this improvement on the electromagnetic sensors. By shifting them back behind the engine air intake, we can free up enough space in the forward compartment for an extra component system."

Alex stopped sketching and waited for Monica's response. When she remained silent, her hair brushing his shoulder as she studied the drawing, he concluded that she hadn't grasped his concept. Sometimes he forgot that she was a project coordinator, not an engineer.

"These two sensors are the only ones that pick up ground-to-air microwave signals," he reminded her. "They are vital to the drone's intelligence-gathering capabilities. But the way they're installed now, they take up more space than necessary."

Monica nodded slowly. "But if you move them farther back in the fuselage," she said, tracing a slender finger across the drawing, "what will that do to weight distribution and signal strength?"

The pencil rolled out of Alex's suddenly slack fingers. He stared at her in astonishment. "Since when have you caught on to the aerodynamic influence of weight distribution?" he inquired.

She stiffened and drew away from him. "I haven't really," she said. "It was just a guess."

"Good girl! We'll make a full-blown engineer out of you yet." Alex had reached over and squeezed her hand before he realized what he was doing. Touching her was like jamming his fingers into a light socket. He drew them back into a clenched fist.

Monica shot off the couch as if she had also felt the electrical charge. She walked away a few paces, her back to him. Alex couldn't see her face, but he was reasonably sure what she was thinking. He had a feeling he was giving off signals like a blinking neon sign—signals that were taboo for both of them, for basically the same reason.

Tom Armstrong was Alex's best friend. For some weeks now, Alex had been increasingly aware that he also might be Tom's best man in the not-too-distant future, thanks to Monica Seabury. He had even been privately rooting for the pair. Until today. *What the hell was happening to him?*

"You flatter me, Alex," Monica told him coolly. "I don't have what it takes to be an aeronautical engineer. Still, I do find your idea interesting."

"Good," Alex said quickly, grateful to be back on safe subject matter. "There's a completed version of the change upstairs in my studio. I just wanted you to have a basic grasp of it before the others get here. Then you can help soften Tom up for me."

She turned, her hands fisted at her sides. "Soften him up?"

"Sure. You know he's going to balk, like always. Especially with the final wind-tunnel test coming up Monday. You *will* help me bring him around, won't you?"

Monica wandered over to the fireplace. Alex studied her profile as she hugged herself for a moment, as if deep in thought, then held her hands out to the crackling fire.

A warm, golden glow washed over her face and highlighted the gentle undulations of her body. Alex mentally combined paints on a palette, trying to decide just what colors he should mix to capture exactly that effect of light and shadow.

"Shouldn't they be here by now?" she asked, without answering his question.

"You know how far it is from Tullahoma," Alex replied. "I figure it'll be another half hour."

Monica rubbed her hands together and moved briskly away from the fireplace. "Well, then—why don't I run upstairs and dig out your pajamas? You'll have plenty of time to change out of those bloody clothes before they get here. Maybe we can fix you up a bed right here on the couch, so you won't have to climb the stairs to your room."

Alex sighed and rubbed his eyes. It was no use. Monica wasn't going to discuss conspiring against

Tom over Shadow. And the effort required to think straight around the blown piston in his skull was too exhausting.

"Scratch the pajamas," he said tersely. He was pretty sure she wouldn't be interested in knowing that he didn't wear them. "Just bring me a clean shirt. I don't want to look like an invalid when they get here. And I'll sleep in my own bed tonight, thank you very much. I've carried Tom home after many a party. It won't hurt him to help me up a few stairs for a change."

To his surprise, Monica offered no objections. She turned and hurried toward the staircase, almost as if he had released her from a trap. Alex stared after her for a moment, then sagged back onto the cushions.

Monica returned a short while later, carrying a red plaid Pendleton shirt on a hanger. "Will this one do?" she asked.

"Fine. Thanks."

She draped the shirt over the back of the couch. Alex fumbled with the buttons on his cuffs. Now that he was horizontal again, he wondered if he could actually muster the energy to change.

"I think I'd better run back up and see if I can repair some of my own damage," Monica said, plucking at her ruined hose.

"Sure. You know where everything is. I guess Joe or Tom can take a hike down to the Porsche and bring up your things later."

Again he got the impression that she was beating a hasty retreat as she headed back toward the staircase. Alex wasn't too incapacitated to have a pretty good idea of what was bugging her.

"Monica, wait up." He rose onto his elbows, determined to clear the air. "I was wrong to try working you into a corner with this thing. What you and Tom have going has nothing to do with Shadow. You have a right to be ticked off at me for trying to use you against him. I promise, it won't happen again."

Her hand came up to finger a chestnut tress from her forehead. "I'm not angry, Alex," she said.

She stood there for a moment longer, while he tried to decide whether she was just being polite. There was something in her voice—an odd tremor of uncertainty. Again Alex sensed vulnerability lurking just behind the steady, gray-blue eyes. While he considered how to deal with that puzzle, Monica turned and disappeared up the stairs.

CHAPTER FOUR

ALEX ABSENTLY FINGERED the bandage on his head as quiet settled over the house. He closed his eyes, and that seemed to quell the nausea caused by the throbbing in his skull. But what helped most was having Monica out of his presence. He was in no condition to try to understand why he felt their simple, businesslike relationship had suddenly become so complex.

In fact, although he hated to admit it, Alex was in no condition for much of anything. The Shadow team would be arriving within the hour, and there was no way that he would be able to play congenial host to them. He almost wished he had let Rafe hang around to run interference for him.

He took a deep breath and sat up slowly, keeping his eyes closed. He couldn't believe he had stood out there in the clearing and let a tree fall on him. He didn't need this, particularly with Shadow so close to completion.

The changes he had come up with for the drone excited Alex, in spite of the headache. They were on the verge of a major breakthrough with the experimental aircraft, and everyone involved had been charged up with adrenaline for weeks. He wanted the key players to be at their peak for next week's wind-tunnel tests, and so a weekend break at Pinehaven had seemed to be just the ticket.

Alex frowned, wondering if he was putting too much stock in their being such a closely knit group. He wasn't ordinarily a suspicious person, but the very nature of Shadow was making him a little paranoid about security.

His fingers drifted to the bandage. Vaguely he seemed to remember watching the tree fall harmlessly to one side. Or had it been one of several others he had cut at the clearing that afternoon?

He was pondering that with growing interest, when the blare of a car horn grabbed his attention. He could hear car doors slamming out front, followed by familiar voices.

Monica was still upstairs, trying to get cleaned up. He hoped Rafe had left the front door unlocked when he left. At the moment, Alex felt welded to the couch.

The front door opened. Nobody had bothered to knock, so he knew Tom had decided to come, after all. Tom had been lukewarm about Pinehaven all week, because of Monica. He would be relieved to learn that she had shown up.

"You'd think he'd have at least left the porch light on for us," Tom said loudly from the entryway.

"Or a candle in the window," Dorie Pryor added, a notch louder.

"Or meet us at the door, as if he were halfway glad to see us," said Joe Anderson, almost shouting.

"Let's be civilized, people," Adelaide suggested, her tone understated and voice controlled. "If Alex knew how you all behaved at the delicatessen in Brevard, he'd have locked you out."

Alex could have sworn he heard one of them blow a raspberry that was followed by good-natured laughter. The foursome crowded through the doorway into the living room, and he was relieved to see that even Adelaide was smiling. She was always the last to let her hair down.

They spotted him slouched on the couch and stopped. Alex braced himself, watching their animated expressions suddenly wash out as their collective gaze fixed on his bandage.

"Good God, Alex!" Tom exclaimed, breaking from the pack and striding rapidly toward him. "What the hell happened?"

"Nothing serious," Alex replied, trying to fake nonchalance. "I was felling the last of the trees for the new helicopter pad, and one of them caught me looking the other way."

Tom whistled through his teeth. He put his hands on his knees and peered into Alex's eyes. Feeling oddly embarrassed, Alex started to get up. Tom placed a restraining hand firmly upon his shoulder.

"No, you don't, old buddy," Tom told him, his gaze shifting to the bandage as the rest of the group gathered around the couch. "You don't look like you can even see straight. How did you do such a good job with the dressing?"

"I didn't." Alex pointed at the ceiling. "Monica."

Tom's eyes widened. He straightened and took a step back, glancing toward the staircase.

"Oh?" He tried visibly to match Alex's nonchalance and failed even more miserably. "How long has she been here?"

"Just long enough to find me out cold," Alex reassured him, taken aback by the hint of jealousy in Tom's voice. "She and Rafe helped me back up here from the clearing."

"Does that sound suspicious, or what?" Dorie declared melodramatically. "A tree falls on our leader, and *poof!*—Monica just happens to pop out of the forest."

Alex squinted up at her. Dorie smirked, which was a whole lot more of a reaction than he was able to muster. Then she bit her lips and inquired, "You *are* all right, aren't you?"

"I'm not dead," he said, needing a break. His performance, pathetic though it must seem to them, was wearing him out. "Can't we save all this concern for my wake?"

Adelaide took her cue and turned upon the group, flapping her hands at them as if shooing chickens. "You heard Alex," she said, taking command. "Let's go bring in our things from the cars."

Joe and Dorie stiffened, saluted Adelaide, did a crisp about-face, and marched toward the door in lockstep as if they had practiced the routine many times. Adelaide looked profoundly annoyed as she followed them out.

"Where did Dorie find that joker?" Tom asked in an undertone, watching them go.

"You've got me there," Alex said, slouching deeper into the cushions and leaning his head back. "But you have to admit, they're a perfect match."

Tom helped himself to the arm of the couch, where Rafe had sat earlier. Alex closed his eyes and sighed heavily, feeling no need for pretense with Tom.

"I'd take you down to the doctor in Brevard," Tom said, "but I'd probably have to hog-tie you first."

"That's right."

They fell silent. Alex waited him out. They had known each other so long that he knew just where Tom would head next.

"Where's Monica's Porsche?" Tom asked.

"Stuck on the old logging road," Alex told him. He felt Tom's weight shift on the couch arm and added, "No, I have no idea what possessed her to try that route. But I am curious. Dumb stunts aren't Monica's style."

He expected Tom to charge upstairs to her. When he didn't, Alex opened one eye and looked at him. Tom sat staring into space, his lips tight. Obviously he was still stung that Monica had taken her badly timed leave of absence without even telling him. Now she had dropped back into the picture—again without contacting Tom. Alex opened his other eye and sat up straight, feeling Tom's pain. Monica had some serious explaining to do.

"Thomas, look here," he said, bringing up a safer topic. "I've come up with a change in the drone's load distribution."

Tom looked at him sharply. Alex reached for his pencil stub again and kept talking as he scribbled on the pad, trying to forestall Tom's objections, at least until he had a chance to present his own case. "The change would require adjustments in the software," he added moments later. "Maybe even a new computer model. Adelaide and Dorie can handle that in plenty of time for the wind-tunnel tests next week."

Tom rose abruptly, a scowl distorting his handsome face. "No way, Alex," he said, emphatically. "It's too late for changes."

"Come on, Tom. As they say in the opera, it ain't over until the fat lady sings. And she doesn't sing until we switch on the blowers in the wind tunnel."

"You don't understand," Tom said, lowering his voice. "Just before we left Tullahoma, I learned that Weissman Aircraft is out to beat us into production with a drone similar to Shadow. If we muff the wind-tunnel test, they could grab the government contract right out from under us."

Alex pursed his lips and nodded. "Let them try. I'm confident that Monday's test will blow them away."

"It might, if we don't start tinkering with the design."

"Trust me, Thomas. The change is important."

"Alex, I said it's too late. There's no way Adelaide and Dorie can handle this on such short notice."

"Handle what?" Adelaide asked.

Alex looked up as Tom spun around. Adelaide stood in the doorway, holding an overnight bag the size of a small suitcase. They heard the front door close, and Dorie and Joe appeared behind her.

"A last-minute design change." Alex eyed Joe.

Adelaide didn't need to be reminded that Joe was an outsider, which meant there would be no discussion of specifics regarding Shadow in his presence. She, as well as the others, had found when it came to weekend breaks it was easier to exercise a little caution in their discussions when Joe was around than to deal with Dorie's attacks of separation anxiety when she had to leave him behind. Adelaide considered Alex's comment for a few seconds, then shifted her gaze to Tom.

"Of course we can handle that, Alex," she said confidently, sounding mildly offended that Tom should have doubts. "Do you want us back to Tullahoma tonight?"

Dorie groaned. "We just got here."

"And here you'll stay," Alex told her. "I want all of you fresh and alert Monday morning. You can get an early start, and Tom will still have time to make the mechanical changes before the test."

Adelaide took a chair. Tom remained standing, one fist clenched at his side. Alex had anticipated some resistance from him. But ordinarily, Tom didn't fight a decision once it had been made.

"It'll work, Tom," Alex said, not understanding why his friend was being so stubborn.

Tom glanced at the stairway and suddenly Alex got the picture. Upset over Monica, Tom was transferring his frustration to the Shadow project. Alex hoped the pair could work out their problems over the next two days. Harmony among the team members was vital for the coming week.

Joe placed a pyramid of delicatessen containers on a narrow parson's table near the door, and Alex fingered his bandage distractedly. Closing his eyes, he had a clear mental image of the tree crashing to the ground several feet away—*and then* of a sharp pain. And of Monica's lips.

His eyes popped open. Tom was the only one looking at him. Alex returned his impenetrable gaze, feeling inexplicably guilty.

GAIL HUNG BACK at the top of the staircase, wondering crazily if Elizabeth Taylor had ever felt this kind of stage fright. She rubbed her sweaty palms together as she listened to the voices down in the living room. She had to force herself to descend, taking the steps slowly, trying to calm her pounding heart.

They spotted her when she was halfway down. Gail froze, trying to smile as she matched faces to the photos from the Shadow game book. Adelaide Barber sat squarely in a big armchair, as if it were a throne. Near the door, the willowy Dorie Pryor was sorting through a prodigious collection of deli containers. Standing beside her was the slightly shorter Joe Anderson. Alex sat hunched on the couch where she had left him, looking pale. Dr. Tom Armstrong was pacing before the stone hearth. When he saw Gail, he stopped and eyed her deliberately.

Nobody spoke. Gail caught herself waiting for someone to make introductions. Shaken by the mental error, recalling how close she had come to giving herself away with Alex earlier, she gritted her teeth and continued down the stairs.

Tom Armstrong met her at the foot of the staircase, his dark eyes intense. "Hello, darling," he murmured, lowering his suntanned face to hers.

Gail instinctively started to draw away as his lips touched hers. Again she caught herself, just in time, and returned his brief kiss. But Tom frowned as their lips parted, and she was certain he had detected her initial hesitation.

Her mind reeling, she glanced around to see how the others had taken his intimate greeting. Only Alex seemed to have taken any notice at all, but his expression was inscrutable. Gail realized with a shock that Tom and her sister had far more than just a working relationship. Why hadn't the Shadow script mentioned that?

"I hear you got stuck on the logging road," Tom said, obviously expecting an explanation.

"It's a long story." Gail managed a nervous laugh to cover her anxiety. She had been too busy impersonating Monica to devise a cover story for her own behavior. "Later?"

Tom paused and nodded reluctantly. Curling an arm around her, he steered her into the room. As she settled into a leather armchair, Tom's fingertips discreetly brushed the side of her breast, sending Gail a jarring message. She sat rigidly, her hands folded in her lap. He sat down on the chair arm, his hand lingering on her shoulder, his thumb tracing tight circles on the back of her neck.

"Alex claims a tree fell on him," Adelaide said, raising one eyebrow.

Swallowing dryly, Gail nodded and glanced at Alex. He stared at the floor, his cheek twitching. She remembered Rafe had mentioned hearing someone or something running in the woods and felt an odd chill.

"Lucky you came along in the nick of time," Dorie commented.

Tom's thumb stopped stroking her neck. Gail sensed that her Monica facade was in danger of crumbling. Everyone—even Alex—was watching her. Feeling that she had absolutely nothing to lose, she risked everything on a shrug.

"Alex is lucky it wasn't a bigger tree," she said.

Dorie and Joe laughed. Tom's thumb resumed its stroking. Gail was light-headed with relief. For the first time, Tom's unfamiliar touch felt good, because it told her that she was still Monica to him. Gail was already acutely aware that the key to her deception lay in his hands.

"What do you think of the project changes, Monica?" Tom asked seriously.

Gail looked up at him. He flicked his gaze toward Joe. She took it as a warning, knowing from the game book that Dorie's boyfriend did not have security clearance.

"Better late than never, I suppose," she said.

Tom didn't look pleased. Alex, on the other hand, seemed relieved. The conflict between the two men over the proposed changes was evident. As assistant project manager, it was Monica's job, and therefore, Gail's, to help make the project work in spite of those differences.

Gail's hand slid into the pocket of Monica's blazer. Her fingers curled around the crumpled note, and she felt again the thrill of anticipation. For the moment that gave her confidence.

"I thought we were all here for a little rest and recreation," she observed. "If we're going to talk shop, we might as well have stayed in Tullahoma."

"Monica is right," Adelaide agreed. "So let's get on with the pig-out. Then, unless Alex decides to work up a high-voltage yen for me, I'm going to turn in early. I want to be up and down to the river before the mist rises, to try out my new Minolta."

Alex squinted at her with one eye and said, "Sweet dreams, Adelaide."

"I keep telling you, Alex," Adelaide retorted dryly, "I'm not going to wait for you forever."

Alex feigned gratitude in the look he gave her. She gazed at him coldly. Then they both winked. She patted him on the shoulder before heading for the makeshift buffet that Joe and Dorie had set up on the parson's table.

"I guess I'd better hike down to my car and fetch my things," Gail said, rising to follow in Adelaide's determined wake.

"I'll go," Tom said, then quickly amended his offer. "We'll go together. Moonlight, the smell of conifers, and you."

Dorie looked up from a carton of crab salad and elbowed Joe. "Did you hear that, Joe? Why don't we go, too?"

"Eat, Dorie," Adelaide commanded, handing her a paper plate.

"You heard the straw boss," Tom said, and ushered Gail out the door.

Gail shivered as they stepped onto the wide porch. Alone with Dr. Tom Armstrong was the last place she wanted to be. As he pulled the door closed and stepped up behind her, she steeled herself for his advances, horribly torn between protecting her virtue and maintaining Monica's clearly amorous interests.

He put his arm around her and they stood on the dark porch, breathing the crisp mountain air. It was a beautiful autumn night in the Smokies, with no wind and just a speckling of stars in the black velvet sky.

"Are you all right, darling?" he asked quietly.

"Sure," she said, then hesitated. "Just a few scrapes on my legs from the underbrush. But I am pooped."

She hoped to keep him at bay by begging fatigue. Tom turned her in his arms to face him. Gail shivered again. Apparently thinking she was cold, he tightened his embrace.

"I wasn't talking about today," he said. "I was referring to why you left without telling me."

Gail felt as if she were stepping into quicksand. She didn't know how to answer him. "It's a long story," she began, then cringed inside, remembering that she had already used that cop-out.

"You've always said I was a good listener," Tom reminded her gently.

She couldn't see his face in the moonlight. But she could hear the tender concern in his voice and feel the lover's strength in his arms. There was no doubt in her mind that he loved Monica deeply. If for no other reason than their common attachment to her twin, Gail began to like him.

"Another time, Tom," she said, and reached up to touch his cheek for Monica.

He bent quickly and covered her lips with his. Gail squeezed her eyes shut and made herself return his kiss, terrified of giving herself away. His knuckles moved slowly down her spine, and she found herself thinking of Alex and the sensuous portrait of Monica.

Tom suddenly released her. She sensed his agitation as he stood with his hands on her shoulders, his fingers digging into her back. Alex had kissed her, too, although she was sure he didn't remember. She could not figure out how Monica fitted into the picture with both men.

"Okay, if that's the way it is," Tom said hoarsely. "I'll wait until we can talk this out. But dammit, you know how hard it is for me to keep my hands off you."

Gail nodded, her voice caught in her throat. She took a deep breath, praying she wouldn't say anything that Monica would regret later. She didn't have a clue as to how she would cope with Alex Shepard's confusingly veiled magnetism—and Tom Armstrong's hungry hands. She had agreed to step into Monica's shoes, but hadn't bargained for any of this.

"Well, I can see I'm getting short-shrifted at every turn this evening," Tom said, an edge on his voice. "Isn't that your suitcase?"

Gail turned. Monica's leather and canvas suitcase stood in the shadows on the bottom step. "Rafe must have brought it up," she said, grateful to the boy. She hadn't looked forward to the long moonlit walk down to the Porsche with Tom.

"He's a good kid, thanks to Alex," Tom commented. He retrieved the suitcase, then stood looking at her. Finally he sighed. "Come on, babe. Let's see if they've left us any of that chow."

He opened the door for her. Gail stepped back inside, feeling as if she was passing from the wolf's lair to the lion's den.

"I'M REALLY BUSHED," Adelaide said groggily, drawing the blanket up around her chin, her gray-flecked hair tucked into a net.

"Join the club." Gail opened her suitcase on the foot of her bed and pulled out Monica's nightgown and robe.

"We came close today, didn't we?" Adelaide observed with a yawn.

"To what?"

"To seeing Shadow go down the tubes." Adelaide punched her pillow to make it fatter. "Alex could have been killed."

Gail's skin prickled at the thought. "Surely not even that would have stopped Shadow at this late date."

"Monica, you *are* tired." Adelaide turned over and drew up a corner of the sheet to shield her eyes from the bedside lamp's muted light.

Gail waited for Adelaide to say more. But when the woman's breathing grew more audible, Gail gave up and took her night clothes into the bathroom. When she emerged several minutes later, her roommate was actually snoring. Feeling restless and keyed up, Gail knew she would never be able to get to sleep, so she stepped into the hallway and silently drew the door shut. She considered going downstairs. But she could hear Alex and Tom still talking down there, and knew she wasn't up to facing either of them again.

Instead she wandered across to Alex's studio and touched the light switch. A soft glow filled the room. Gail moved over the hardwood floor on bare feet, quietly examining the unframed paintings leaning against the walls. Most of them were landscapes. Alex had a fine touch with a brush. She drifted slowly from painting to painting, drawn deeper and deeper into the mountain vistas, sometimes peering through boughs of green conifers, sometimes bathing her mind in the cooling waters of the French Broad River.

She was jolted from her reverie by the unscenic obstacle of the drafting table. Gail blinked as she realized she was looking at a detailed diagram of Shadow for the first time. She reached up and switched on the high-intensity light over the table, enthralled by the spectacular simplicity of the design.

"Yes, Monica," she whispered, noting the penciled-in alterations, still vividly aware of the oil paintings lining the studio. "Alex Shepard is—something else."

Gail remained lost in the Shadow diagram until the overhead track lighting suddenly blinked off, then on. She spun around, startled. Alex stood in the doorway, leaning heavily on Tom, his hand on the light switch.

"We thought everyone was asleep by now," Tom said.

Although neither man seemed disturbed to find her prowling around in Alex's studio, Gail felt a need to explain herself. "Adelaide snores," she said.

"Why doesn't that surprise me?" Alex asked, and both men smiled wryly. Alex moved away from Tom and shuffled to the drafting table. "Come here, Thomas. Let me show you how simple this design change will be."

Tom joined them, casually hooking a finger around the belt of Gail's robe. Suddenly aware of her attire, Gail pulled the collar of the robe snugly around her throat. Tom used all the body language of intimate familiarity around her. But she couldn't help reminding herself that it was Alex who possessed the astoundingly sensuous portrait of Monica.

"Monica, my friend," Alex said, scowling darkly. "You know how I hate having my sketches tampered with."

"I haven't touched anything, Alex," she assured him.

"You didn't remove these?" Alex picked loose thumbtacks from the metal catch plate at the bottom of the board, and carefully replaced them along the edge of the Shadow diagram.

"No." Gail glanced up at Tom as he let go of her belt. Was he noticing something about her? Something that was not Monica?

Tom shrugged. "Maybe Adelaide was having a look at it," he suggested.

"Or Dorie—or *Joe*," Alex said pointedly. "It was stupid of me to leave it out like this, knowing an outsider would be in the house."

He rubbed his eyes, looking so distressed that without thinking, Gail reached out and touched his arm. She drew her hand away at once, aware both of the surge of excitement generated by the contact and of the effect of her action on Tom. Trying to repair the damage, she stepped to one side so that Tom stood between Alex and herself.

"Take it easy, Alex," Tom said, taking a closer look at the diagram. "This is just the old plain vanilla, Model-T workup. If it showed up on the front page of the *New York Times*, it wouldn't be any great loss. Assuming, of course, that you've kept the crown jewels safely stashed.''

''I have.'' Alex leaned against the drawing board. ''Do you mind doing the honors, Tom? I'd just as soon not have to bend over.''

Tom rolled a rubber-castered paint supplies cart to one side, and carefully stepped on a section of hardwood floorboards. The spring-loaded section popped up when he removed his foot, revealing a safe below. Tom got down on hands and knees to work the combination lock. Opening the thick, fireproof door, he reached inside and withdrew a sheaf of papers.

''We'll need just the top one,'' Alex said.

Tom peeled off the top sheet and tacked it over the diagram on the drawing board. Scanning the newest version of Shadow, he scowled, and Gail could see his jaw muscles bunch.

Still shaking his head in disgust with himself, Alex picked up a drafting pencil and tapped the diagram. ''Tom, you can see what I was talking about here.'' He pointed out the penciled alterations he had made, explaining the shift in Shadow's microwave sensors.

Gail listened, enthralled, as she had when he had explained it to her earlier. She leaned closer. The penciled alterations were only roughed-in, like incomplete thoughts. But they were clear enough so that Gail could easily complete them herself in her mind.

"It won't work," Tom said, when Alex finished. "With the sensors moved back there, engine heat will interfere."

Seeing precisely what Alex was getting at, Gail plucked the drafting pencil from his hand. "Put a heat-resistant carbon-fiber-reinforced shield here," she suggested drawing a line against the forward end of the component, "and you solve that problem."

The two men stared at the diagram for a long moment. Then their heads turned in unison toward Gail. The pencil rolled from her fingers as she took in their expressions. With a terrible sinking sensation, Gail realized that she had done it again.

"Don't laugh, guys," she stammered, thinking as she spoke that laughter appeared to be the thing farthest from their minds. "I'm bound to get lucky and make a right guess now and then."

"Is that what it was?" Tom asked. "A guess?"

Gail smiled, frantically searching for an escape hatch. She found it in the look in Alex's eyes. "Okay, I confess. Alex told me about it earlier."

Alex looked surprised, then confused. "Did I?"

"For heaven's sake, Alex," she said, forging ahead, trying to keep him off balance. "If you can't remember what you told me two hours ago you ought to be in bed. You're playing around with that concussion, and it's dangerous."

Tom looked at Alex with concern. Following through on her advantage, Gail reached up and switched off the light over the drafting table.

"I don't know about you, but I'm out of gas," she said. "Snoring or no snoring, I'm going to turn in."

She started for the door. As an afterthought, she retraced her steps and gave Tom a peck on the cheek. He smiled reflexively. Gail hurried out of the studio, barely able to resist looking at Alex.

Back in the room she shared with Adelaide, she leaned against the door, her heart pounding. Had she really covered her slip? Or were Alex and Tom putting pieces together right now to form a picture that was not Monica? She pressed her ear to the wood panel and heard Tom's muffled voice, whispering as he walked with Alex down the hallway toward the master bedroom. A short while later, a single set of footsteps returned, paused outside Gail's door and passed on.

Alone with the sound of Adelaide's strident snoring, Gail moved toward her own bed. Exhausted by the strain, she was eager to crawl between the sheets and put an end to her first anxiety-ridden day as Monica. She grabbed hold of the suitcase and started to lift it off the foot of her bed. Something made her stop.

A wisp of white lace protruded from one side. Gail slowly raised the zippered lid. Earlier, when she had first opened the suitcase, her clothes—Monica's clothes—had been folded and packed with the precision of a shirt factory. Now they looked rumpled, as if someone had hurriedly groped through them, then tried to put them back the way they were.

Gail sucked in her breath. Who had been curious enough about her to riffle through her luggage? It almost had to have been Dorie or Joe, or maybe Adelaide. But why? Had one of them seen through her deception? Who could she turn to? Certainly not Alex or Tom—not without risking her cover. Gail slid the suitcase onto the floor, slipped off her robe, and got into bed. She turned off the lamp on the bedside table. But it was a long time before she slept.

CHAPTER FIVE

"HOW COULD YOU OVERSLEEP, dummy?" Gail whispered to herself, hurriedly slipping into Monica's blue slacks.

She had drifted awake only minutes earlier, floating on the tail end of her recurrent dream. For once, the indistinct vision of a childhood mirror self had not left her with a feeling of vague emptiness. This time, knowing that today she would be reunited with her twin, Gail had bolted from bed with soaring anticipation.

Adelaide was already long gone, her bed made up with military precision. For a large woman who snored like a grizzly bear, Adelaide could be church mouse quiet when she wanted to, Gail thought.

Tugging on a sweater, she stuffed Monica's note into her pocket and quickly left the room. She knew she should destroy the slip of paper. But she couldn't bring herself to relinquish the fragile link with her sister.

Tripping down the stairs, she followed the smell of coffee through the living room and along a short hallway to the kitchen. Gail didn't know how she was going to manage to get away to Brevard alone for her meeting with Monica. With a glance at her watch, she realized she didn't have much time to come up with a plan, either.

"Good morning, sleepyhead," Alex greeted her, as she burst into the kitchen. He sat at a plank table, his hands locked around a big pottery mug.

Gail felt a rush of warmth as their eyes met. He held her gaze just a beat longer than necessary, then reached for a thermos pitcher that stood on the table.

"You look better this morning," she said, watching him pour a second mug of coffee and slide it toward her.

"So do you. Yesterday I thought you were twins."

Gail froze. Then it occurred to her that Alex meant he had been seeing double. But that didn't ease her mind. This morning he was getting a good look at her for the first time.

At the moment, however, he seemed more concerned with the contents of the sugar bowl. Holding it out to her he asked, "Is there enough here to satisfy your rabid sweet tooth?"

Obviously Monica drank her coffee heavily laced with sugar. Gail smiled, hoping her stomach wouldn't revolt as she spooned sugar into her cup. She forced herself not to grimace as she sipped the beverage.

"Where is everyone?" she asked.

"The whole bunch trumped up a canoe trip down the French Broad. They'll be gone all day." Alex eyed her thoughtfully.

Gail was about to express disappointment that she had missed out on the trip, when he added, "Tom knew you'd rather be flogged than tackle the great outdoors. He said to tell you he'd make it up to you when they got back."

Gail struggled to keep her expression bland. Tom seemed to have seized on the canoe trip as a way to put distance between Monica and himself. *He's acting out his frustration over my behavior,* she thought. From the studious manner in which Alex was watching her, Gail surmised that he was thinking the same thing.

She let her relief show, hoping he would take it as Monica's response to being left out of the canoe trip, even as she acknowledged her first major difference from her twin. Next to Monica's aversion to the outdoors, her sweet tooth seemed insignificant.

"By the way, Rafe's father has gone into town for a tow truck," Alex told her. "Rafe says the oil pan is punctured on your Porsche. The foreign-car garage in Brevard can have it repaired by this afternoon."

"I really need to get into town myself," Gail said, trying not to sound too eager. "I need to pick up a few things—and make sure the mechanic doesn't soak me.''

Alex drained his mug and clomped it down onto the table. "Well, *I* like Pinehaven, even if the rest of you appear to have better places to spend the weekend.''

Before Gail could apologize for abandoning him for the morning, Alex shoved himself up and out of his chair. He tottered slightly, blinking. She started toward him, but he waved her off.

"Just a little eye problem,'' he said. "Comes and goes.''

"You shouldn't be up and around.''

Alex dug into his pocket and tossed her a key ring. "Scat. I don't need another mama at my age.''

Gail could stand there and argue with him, or she could be on her way to Brevard and Monica. She was out of the kitchen and heading for the front door with hardly a second thought.

She was clattering down the porch steps before she realized Alex was following her. As he ambled onto the porch to lean against the railing, she came to a dead stop. She had no idea which of the three vehicles parked on the east side of the cabin went with the key he had given her. Hoping for a clue, she peeked at the key. Toyota Motor. Not much help, Gail thought to herself, noting that two of the three cars were Toyotas. Hoping she was choosing the right one, she headed past the smaller compact, opened the door of the four-wheel-drive vehicle and climbed inside. When she saw leather seats and a jazzy disc player, she was sure she had blown it. She held her breath, inserted the key and gave it a twist. The engine growled to life and Gail moaned with relief.

Minutes later she pulled onto the highway. A smoky haze lay over the mountains in the distance, and Gail felt her excitement mounting as each dip and turn in the road led her closer to Brevard and Monica, so that by the time she pulled into the motel parking lot, she was trembling. Parking at the side of the building, she got out and walked down a chilly breezeway to Room 209, her heels clacking on the pavement. She raised her hand to knock, and the door swung open.

They stared at each other in stunned silence. Gail felt the blood drain from her own face as she watched it leave Monica's.

"May I come in?" Gail asked lamely.

Monica stepped back quickly, her jaw snapping shut. Gail moved past her into a shabby little room smelling of musty carpet and disinfectant. Monica eased the door shut. Still they stared at each other, aware of nothing beyond the three feet of space separating them.

Monica suddenly laughed. The sound was so like Gail's that tears sprang from her eyes. With the ice broken, they were suddenly in each other's arms, laughing and crying, clinging to the distant glimmer of their briefly shared past.

"My sister," Gail whispered, choked with joy. "There is so much to talk about."

"And so little time," Monica said, squeezing Gail hard before drawing away.

"I don't know where to start." Gail followed Monica's lead, crawling onto the bed. They sat facing each other, still spellbound by their physical sameness.

"Not at the beginning," Monica went on in a somber tone. "If we don't concentrate on *now*, we might never have a future."

Gail reached into her pocket and pulled out the crumpled note. "How did you know I'd get mixed up in this? And that I'd be wearing the suede jacket yesterday?"

"Dick Brady," Monica said flatly. "You're here, so I know you two have met. As far as I know, he's the only other person who knows about us—except maybe for some obscure clerk in the National Security Agency's records-keeping section."

Gail started to mention Howard Eastman, but Monica hurried on.

"I found out about you quite by accident. I was in Dick's office four days ago and opened a file with my name on it that was lying on his desk. There were a couple of photos of me. There was one that puzzled me. I was wearing a dress I didn't recognize. In fact, I knew I'd never owned it. I confronted Dick and he told me about you. He also said you might be a handy ace in the hole if ever I needed a backup. I told him I wouldn't stand for it. But I was abducted before I could contact you, and I had an idea Dick might rope you into helping him save the Shadow project." Monica slammed a fist against her thigh in exasperation. "Bringing you into this mess was so stupid, Gail. I told Dick to keep you out of my work, no matter what, but he obviously didn't listen to me."

"Abducted?" Gail rocked back, holding her knees.

Monica nodded. "Sounds crazy, doesn't it? I was on my way to a meeting with Dick, when some cockeyed stooge grabbed me. Scared the willies out of me. I don't know where he planned to take me, because we never got there. I managed to slip away when he stopped at a service station.

"A couple of days later, I risked returning to my apartment in Tullahoma. If Dick used you, it was logical that he would provide you with my clothes and things. So I left the note in my suede jacket, which I wear a lot, and left the jacket lying out on the bed. I could only hope that no one else would come across the note, and that you would find it in time."

"Why haven't you gone to the police?" Gail asked.

Monica looked down at her hands, and Gail could almost feel her thinking. When Monica looked at her again, her smoky-blue eyes were brimming.

"If it was just me, I *would* go to the police, Gail. But this situation is too mixed-up. I'm not sure who had me kidnapped or why, but it almost certainly has to do with the Shadow project. I don't know who can be trusted—even the police. And I won't make any move that might endanger my—baby."

Gail's mouth dropped open. "Monica, I'm an *aunt*?"

Monica smiled wearily, placing a hand over her abdomen. "Not yet. But we're getting there."

Gail threw her arms around Monica's neck and hugged her. Then the beautiful portrait of her sister flashed into Gail's mind, and she forced herself to seek an answer that oddly enough, she dreaded.

"Who is the father?" she asked.

"Tom Armstrong," Monica replied without hesitation. "Only he doesn't know yet, so you mustn't let on. I was planning to surprise him, after the pressure of the Shadow tests was over."

Gail let out her breath through pursed lips. "Why didn't Brady tell me you were involved with Tom?"

"Dick doesn't know. Falling in love while on the job isn't considered very professional conduct within the agency."

"Will, uh, Tom be my brother-in-law someday?" Gail asked haltingly.

Monica nodded. "Before everything got messed up, we were thinking about a Thanksgiving wedding."

"Mmm—Monica—he sort of, well, kissed me."

Monica's expression sharpened. "Oh?" She thought about it for a moment. "Did you kiss him back?"

"For you. But no more than I had to."

Monica's face reddened, and Gail braced herself for an angry explosion. Instead, her twin suddenly doubled over with laughter.

"I can't believe you could fool Tom, Gail," she said, recovering and wiping her eyes.

"Maybe he's partially blinded by love," Gail suggested. "But I can tell he senses something isn't right, so I'm trying to stay away from him as much as possible."

The romantic portrait in Pinehaven's master bedroom again intruded upon Gail's thoughts. Now, more than ever, it didn't make sense.

"Monica," she said, approaching the subject cautiously, "did Alex ever paint your picture?"

Monica looked aghast. "Why on earth would he want to?"

"No reason," Gail said quickly. Part of her was relieved as she plunged deeper into confusion. "He strikes me as being an extremely talented artist."

"Yes, for a workaholic." Monica squirmed off her side of the bed and began pacing the room. "How about Alex? How was my sudden disappearance explained?"

"You left a note requesting a leave of absence, thanks to Brady."

"I'll bet that went over like a lead balloon."

"Tom is upset—hurt," Gail told her. "I keep putting off explaining my—*your* absence, because I haven't come up with anything he'd buy. But Alex mostly just seems relieved to have you back. But then, he was unconscious when I first met him."

Monica stopped pacing and stared at her. Gail explained about finding Alex in the clearing, and helping Rafe get him back up to the cabin.

"You see what I've been getting at," Monica resumed, sinking back onto the bed as if her legs wouldn't hold her. "First I'm abducted. Then Alex is assaulted."

"He says a tree fell on him."

"Did it?" Monica didn't wait for an answer. "Alex isn't that careless. No, Gail. Happening this week, that's just too much of a coincidence."

"Why would anyone want to hurt him—or you?"

"Shadow." Monica spoke the word as if it explained everything. "Someone is trying to stop it."

"Who?"

Monica shrugged and stared into space. "I thought I had that figured out. Now I don't know."

"Who did you think it was?"

"I have no proof, Gail. And if I tell you who I suspect and that person turns out to be innocent, you might let your guard down around the real culprit. That could be dangerous for you."

"Someone inside Shadow?"

"Possibly. *Probably.*"

They looked at each other, and neither had to say what each was clearly thinking: for the time being, Gail was Monica. That put Gail on the list, too.

"Are you going through with it?" Monica inquired.

Gail wanted to say no. But she couldn't just go back to Martindale and pretend none of this had happened. She couldn't leave Monica hiding out, with no one else to turn to. And what about Alex? If someone was out to kill the Shadow project—*kill!* —wasn't Alex the obvious target? She shivered slightly. Then she forced herself to set aside her emotions. Without Monica—without Alex—would she still stick it out? Shadow technology could play a major role in national defense in the years to come. As a scientist, she could not turn her back on the responsibility she had accepted when she agreed to play a part in this charade.

"I have to," she said finally.

"I'm afraid for you, Gail," Monica told her, smiling slightly as she took Gail's hands. "I'm also very proud of you."

They held each other for a long moment, wet cheeks pressed together. Gail ached inside. This was all so unfair. In a way, fate was punishing them for being sisters. A million questions crowded in upon her—twenty-six years' worth of questions. But Monica had been right: there was so little time.

Gail looked at her watch and couldn't believe it was so late. "Oh, Monica, I have to go!" she exclaimed, anguished.

Monica started to protest, then stopped herself. She lifted her chin and looked deeply into Gail's eyes. "For now," she said.

"For now," Gail repeated. She glanced around the shabby room. "Do you need anything? Money?"

Monica hesitated, and that was enough. Gail grabbed her purse and emptied her billfold onto the bed. Dick Brady had been generous with pocket money.

"Take all of this," Gail said. "I can use your credit cards."

"Use the VISA," Monica instructed. "It's billed straight to the NSA's unaudited covert account."

At the door, Monica took Gail's arm. "I'll be leaving right after you, Gail, just in case someone followed you."

Gail was suddenly alarmed at the prospect of again losing contact with her twin. "How will I find you?"

Monica winked. "You won't. Leave the skulking to me. I'll be in touch as soon as you get back to Tullahoma."

They embraced one last time, and Gail forced herself out the door. She hurried through the breezeway to Alex's 4 Runner and drove around to the motel entrance. She was about to pull onto the highway, when a tow truck roared past.

Gail spotted Rafe in the passenger seat, a split second before she saw Monica's Porsche hiked up on the tow chain. Gail waited for a moment after the rig had passed, convincing herself that Rafe hadn't noticed her sitting there in Alex Shepard's vehicle, idling at the entrance to the seedy Mountain Park Motel. Then she turned onto the highway to follow the tow truck to the garage.

"MISS SEABURY, do you paint?" Rafe asked, as Gail turned under the rustic sign at the entrance to the steep driveway leading up to Pinehaven.

Gail kept her eyes on the road and made a wild guess. "No. But I'd like to someday."

"Alex is teaching me." Rafe grinned, and an unmistakable warmth crept into his reedy voice. "He's a good teacher."

Rafe had talked virtually nonstop since they left the foreign-car garage in Brevard. He had mentioned Alex no less than a dozen times, speaking of his own father only once, briefly. As she steered the 4 Runner into the flat parking area beside the cabin, Gail realized that she was growing fond of the boy.

Alex was standing on the broad porch, clad in hiking boots and a light jacket. Gail parked the car where she had found it and got out.

"Just where do you think you're going, Alex?" she asked, marching toward the porch with Rafe at her heels.

"I've got to get out for awhile," Alex said. "Claustrophobia."

Gail stopped on the bottom step and looked up at his half-closed eyes. Suspecting he was still nursing a headache, she began to chide him for being outside at all, so soon after yesterday's accident. He ignored her and turned to Rafe.

"When will the Porsche be ready?"

"By midafternoon," Rafe replied. "The mechanic will deliver it out here when he's finished."

"Good. Did you check on the chopper-pad contractors while you were in town?"

"Yes, sir." Rafe seemed to draw himself up taller. "I phoned all three, just like you said. The earth-moving equipment will be here Monday morning to level the ground. The cement contractor will begin work Tuesday. The electrician should have the cable for the night-landing lights buried by midweek, weather permitting."

Alex came down the steps and shook hands with Rafe, very businesslike. "You're doing a good job."

Rafe beamed, shooting a glance at Gail, obviously thrilled by Alex's approval. Gail smiled back. The boy reminded her of a big-boned puppy, bright-eyed and anxious to please.

"Now, if memory serves me right," Alex said, frowning up at the clear autumn sky, "you have an English Lit. test coming up next week."

Rafe's face fell and his shoulders drooped. Alex pointed toward the woods. Rafe jutted his jaw and scowled. Alex snapped his fingers commandingly and pointed again. Rafe took a deep breath and loosed a howl of adolescent frustration that startled Gail. She watched him spring off, bellowing something about grappling with Shakespeare's ghost.

Alex chuckled. "Go for an A, Rafe," he murmured. "You can do it this time."

"I'm beginning to think that boy can do anything *you* set his mind to," Gail observed.

"Rafe has a lot of potential. All he needs is direction." Alex poked his hands into his jacket pockets. "And all I need is a walk in the fresh air."

"You can't go alone, Alex. Not in your condition."

"My condition is fine." He tilted his head to one side. "You aren't suggesting you'd like to come along, are you, Monica?"

Monica. Gail felt trapped between her desire to explore Pinehaven at Alex's side and the knowledge of Monica Seabury's well-established aversion to the outdoors.

"You can't go alone," she said stubbornly.

"Be damned if you're not thinking about coming with me," he said, clearly bemused. He kept his head canted to one side, the noon sunlight catching in his hair.

Then he turned and strode toward the fringe of conifers surrounding the cabin, walking with the measured gait of an experienced hiker. Gail, still caught in her Monica-Alex-Gail triangle, watched until he was almost out of sight. By the time she'd reasoned that Monica would have set aside her own feelings and followed her sense of duty, Gail had to run to catch up.

Autumn was already nipping leaves from the deciduous trees and scattering pine cones from the towering conifers. Gail walked easily at Alex's side, inhaling the pine-scented air, the fragrance filling her lungs and clearing her senses. Her lean thighs began to tingle, thanks to Alex's steady pace. Soon the bright light, the piny air and the tingling began to send her into a dreamlike trance. Gail envisioned a log burning in the big stone hearth back at the cabin. The log split, sending a flurry of gold dust up the chimney. A man and a woman lay in each other's arms on the deep hearth rug, sharing a glass of wine. The woman—Gail—looked up into the probing eyes of Alex Shepard, even as he drew her nearer.

Gail walked smack into Alex. He grunted and grabbed her. Still under the influence of her daydream, she gasped at the feel of his hands on her arms.

"I said, do you want to rest, Monica?"

Gail looked up at him. Unaware that he had spoken before, she nodded woodenly. She wasn't the least bit tired, but standing there in his powerful grip, her knees were rapidly turning to jelly.

Alex brushed loose bark from a fallen log. They sat down next to each other, and he stretched his long legs on the spongy carpet of pine needles.

"I'm glad you came along." He spoke in a hushed tone, as if reluctant to disturb the quiet of the mountain air.

"Me, too," Gail whispered, gazing up into the sun-glittered treetops. "This is almost like being in a—in a cathedral."

Alex didn't make another sound. After awhile she looked at him. He was staring at her strangely, as if she had just materialized out of nowhere.

"You feel that, too, Monica?" he asked finally.

Monica. Gail stiffened. *Careful,* she warned herself. Her sister wouldn't have enjoyed this rambling hike and certainly wouldn't have seen the cathedral. Having let herself show through again, Gail scurried around in her mind, trying to restore her Monica facade.

"I didn't mean to run into you a minute ago," she said. "I had my mind on Rafe. He wouldn't let me pay him for all the trouble he went to with my car."

"No. He wouldn't." Alex picked up a stick and sat worrying a pinecone on the ground near his boots. "He thinks he owes me something, and he keeps taking it out on my friends."

"Rafe idolizes you, Alex. He told me about the art lessons and math tutoring, and the time you took his little sister to the doctor when she was sick last winter. I can see how he would think he owes you."

Alex shook his head, twirling the pinecone in a circle. "I get more from Rafe than I could ever give," he said with an odd note of sadness.

Gail recognized his loneliness—it was the same kind of yearning that she tried so hard to deny in herself.

"Rafe's had some pretty hard breaks," she commented.

"He told you that?" Alex looked surprised.

"No. Just a guess. He looks old for his age. Kids can get that way when life kicks their childhood in the knees."

Alex nodded. "His mother died a few years back, leaving Rafe and his sister and brothers to more or less fend for themselves. Their old man spends most of his time back in the woods working a moonshine still—and drinking the biggest part of his production. Whatever Rafe gets out of this world, he'll have to grab for himself."

"With a little help from his friends."

Alex snared the pinecone on the end of the stick and handed it to her. Gail accepted it with a grin that he matched. They rose, and she stood cradling the pinecone as if it were something precious.

A breeze sprang up, soughing through the boughs overhead. His hair riffled softly across his wide forehead. Gail recalled exactly how it had felt on her fingertips when she brushed it aside as he lay unconscious the day before. Just before he kissed her.

She licked her lips, swallowing hard. Alex had been gazing down at her with a studious expression that was somehow suspended between a smile and a frown. Now he seemed to rouse himself.

"I'd like to show you what I have in mind for the chopper pad," he said, then smiled ruefully. "That is, if you haven't already seen enough of the clearing."

"Show me," she said, hoping he didn't notice the unsteadiness in her voice. "Believe it or not, I'm actually enjoying the great outdoors."

"I'm glad," he said seriously.

Neither of them moved. Gail began to feel her pulse in the side of her neck. The wind and sun were in his hair, and she was swimming in the soothing depths of his dark eyes.

Alex turned suddenly and moved away at a brisk pace. Gail pulled herself together and followed. He thwacked savagely at the russet and gold underbrush with the stick, almost as if he were angry with himself.

"I hated to cut the trees," he told her quietly as they arrived at the oval-shaped clearing. "But I'll be able to come to Pinehaven more often with the helicopter."

"The opening doesn't look big enough," Gail said.

"This is just for the pad." He drew a big circle in the air with his stick. "I could probably get by with it like this, by making high-performance takeoffs. But hotdog chopper pilots have notoriously short life spans, so Rafe and I will open it up a little more this winter to give the rotor blade more room."

"Amazing," Gail said.

"Huh?" Alex paused, stick in midair.

"Where do you find the time for all this, Alex? You're the father of Shadow, a mother to Rafe, an accomplished artist, outdoorsman, helicopter pilot." Gail threw up her hands. "And what else?"

Alex lowered his arm slowly. The stick fell from his hand. Staring straight at her, his gaze seemed to grow distant and distracted. He took a step toward her and lifted her chin with his fingertips. His dark eyes took in every detail of her face, like an artist examining a model.

Gail's flesh went hot and then cold. Every part of her wanted to respond to his gentle touch—but he was studying her too closely. Fear of what he might be seeing drew an icy finger down her spine.

"You're a beautiful woman, Monica."

Alex straightened with a jerk, as if shocked by the sound of his own voice. He backed away two paces, his expression suddenly guarded, and cleared his throat.

"It's getting late," he said. "We'd better be getting back." With that, he turned and set a rapid pace through the trees toward the cabin.

BACK IN THE SAFETY of her room, Gail stripped off her blouse and slacks, hoping the harsh spray of a shower would wash away her feverish confusion over what had happened between Alex and herself back there in the clearing. Had he really been on the verge of kissing her? But that was impossible. To Alex she was Monica, and Monica was in love with his best friend, Tom Armstrong.

None of that explained the portrait in his bedroom. Could Alex be secretly in love with Monica?

"Oh, what a mess," Gail whispered, shimmying out of her underwear and wrapping a towel around herself. She opened the shower door, turned on the taps, and stepped inside. She felt the steam reach out to her like the warm hands of a lover. With little effort, she envisioned the strong body of her phantom lover joining her under the spray. The lover was Alex. The fragrance of her bath oil filled the small enclosure and increased the sensuous aura of her fantasies.

It was as if she were beginning a long mindless free-fall into the depth of an imagined kiss, and she gasped. "No! Stop it, you idiot!" Trembling, Gail stepped from the shower, wrapped the towel around her body and opened the bedroom door. What had she expected? The room was empty and so was her heart. Still too dazed to think, she turned and eased onto the bed, pulling the spread close around her as if seeking protection.

Sometime later, the door opened. Gail lay perfectly still, her eyes closed, feigning sleep as footsteps quietly approached the bed.

"Monica?" Adelaide whispered.

Monica. Gail kept her eyes shut, and a chill swept through her body. Of course, Alex had believed he'd be kissing Monica. Gail was in danger of falling in love with a man who was apparently drawn to her twin.

She wanted to cry out, to pound her fist into the pillow. Instead she continued to pretend she was asleep, taking the emotional blow on the chin.

Gail felt invisible. Once she stopped being Monica—once this whole crazy Shadow deception ended—as far as Alex Shepard was concerned, Gail Montgomery would cease to exist.

CHAPTER SIX

JUST AFTER NOON the next day, Tom accelerated onto the highway behind the Porsche, then slowed slightly. Gail watched Monica's sports car stretch its lead in front of them, glumly wondering how Dorie could manage to sit so close to Joe in a car with bucket seats.

The sense of remoteness that she had felt throughout the last two restless nights at Pinehaven remained with Gail now, as the Shadow team broke camp and headed back to Tennessee. Tom's insistence that she make the trip with him had only deepened her mood. She had been counting on having this time to herself, sheltered within the cocoon of the Porsche.

Gail peeked sideways at Tom's matinee-idol profile. It made sense for him to want Monica at his side after their long separation. And Joe had jumped at the chance to drive the Porsche back to Tullahoma, rather than ride back in the far less agreeable environs of Adelaide's compact car.

"Monica, I won't bite," Tom said, flicking a glance at the expanse of car seat between them.

Gail reluctantly reduced the distance. When his hand came down off the steering wheel to rest on her thigh, she shivered with apprehension. Unfortunately, Tom took that as the best possible sign and smiled. He pulled her closer until their thighs touched.

Searching desperately for a way to keep him at arm's length while still maintaining body contact, Gail tried to wedge a third person between them. "Do you think Alex should be driving alone today?" she asked.

Tom's smile faded. "He's okay."

Gail wasn't so sure. Alex had rubbed his eyes all through lunch, as if he might be still having vision problems from Friday's concussion. She kept that concern to herself, however, acutely conscious that Tom suspected there was something going on between Alex and Monica.

To Gail's surprise, tears stung at her eyes. She blinked them back and forced herself to place her hand in Tom's.

"Alex seems to have adopted Rafe," she went on, chagrined that she couldn't seem to shoulder Alex back out of the conversation.

Tom's smile returned. "Yeah. He's twisted the arm of an art dealer he knows in Dallas, and the guy's agreed to arrange a small show of Rafe's paintings next spring. Alex thinks that the kid might get a college scholarship on the merit of his art."

"What do you think?" Gail asked.

"I think he'll see that Rafe goes to college, with or without a scholarship." Tom removed his hand from her thigh just long enough to navigate a sharp curve in the highway. "Old Alex is one man who should be married with a dozen kids of his own."

"What about old Tom?" Gail couldn't help it. She had to know how Tom might feel about the baby Monica was carrying—his baby.

"I'm not a family-man type," Tom said. Gail's heart sank, then he added, "I couldn't stand having more than five or six kids around the house."

Gail laughed out loud, delighted for Monica. Tom gave her a crooked grin.

"Hey!" he exclaimed. "My honey is back!"

"I have been kind of a wet blanket for you this weekend, haven't I?"

"A wet blanket is better than no blanket at all, which is what I had last week while you were gone," Tom told her. "Do you think we could talk about that now?"

Gail froze up inside, angry with herself for allowing the conversation to veer offtrack into quicksand. Of the dozen excuses she had managed to think up, not one seemed the least bit believable at the moment.

"Please, Tom," she said. "Trust me—and wait."

He drove on in silence for a while. Finally he said, "Just tell me one thing, Monica. Does it have something to do with Alex?"

Hearing the dread in his voice, Gail rushed to correct his misconception. "No, Tom." She leaned forward, so she could look him in the face. "This has absolutely nothing to do with Alex."

Tom reached out and drew Gail under his arm. She felt warmth for Monica's lover—this man who had enough faith in Gail's sister to trust her blindly.

They were past the twisting, dipping roads of the deep Smokies now. The highway stretched flat before them between the low-lying foothills on the Tennessee side of the mountains. Tom shifted the seat back to make more room for his long legs, and set the car's cruise control.

"I'll be damned glad when Shadow is in the bag," he remarked.

"Me, too." Gail spoke from the heart. Then, resting her head upon Tom's shoulder, she pretended to sleep. It seemed the easiest way to avoid an uncomfortable situation.

When they reached the outskirts of Tullahoma two hours later, Tom nudged her upright. "From the looks of the trees, there's been an early frost," he said, flexing his shoulder.

"I love this time of year." This time Gail caught herself before blurting that she liked to walk in the woods and hear crisp autumn leaves crunching beneath her feet. "I wish I liked the outdoors as much as you do, Tom."

He turned down a short street. Glimpsing the sign, Gail realized he was heading straight for Monica's apartment complex, located at the end of the cul-de-sac. Tom pulled into a parking lot, whipped the car into a numbered slot and killed the motor.

"It's good to be home," she said, and the statement sounded empty, even to her ears.

"Don't forget Adelaide's pizza party this evening."

Gail opened her door to cover her surprise. She hadn't heard about any get-togethers at Adelaide's. The news set her teeth on edge. Being trapped in the car with Tom all afternoon had left her desperate for time alone.

"I'm done in, Tom. I'm going to skip Adelaide's."

Tom folded his forearms on the steering wheel and rested his forehead on his wrists. Gail knew she had made a wrong choice, but there were no right ones. What was right for Tom was wrong for her.

He threw open his door with an air of resignation. Gail got out, too, and pulled Monica's heavy suitcase from the back seat. Tom came around and took it from her, and she let him lead the way across the parking lot.

She tried not to rubberneck as she took in the covered swimming pool and the carefully manicured hedges, all surrounded by a high brick privacy wall. She followed Tom up a short flight of stairs into the apartment building's lobby. A quick elevator ride later, they stepped into a wide hallway.

When he stopped at the last door on the left, Gail began rummaging in her purse for the key. He pulled out his own key ring, sorted through its four keys, slipped one into the lock and held the door open for her. Gail tried not to show her surprise.

Stepping inside, she had to stifle a gasp of pleasure. The spacious living room was furnished in her favorite colors.

Tom dropped the suitcase next to the door and crossed the plush pile carpet. Gail joined him at the wide window that overlooked a brick courtyard. They stood in silence, looking down at the border plantings of bronze and yellow chrysanthemums.

"I love you," he said after awhile.

"I'm glad." Gail felt as if she were walking a tightrope without a safety net. For Monica she added, "You're my life, Tom."

Before she knew what was happening, she was in Tom's arms, and he was kissing her with the passion she had been fearing all day. Gail returned his kiss mechanically, in a near panic. Suddenly he released her and stepped back, hands on hips.

"Am I really your life, Monica?" he asked, his eyes narrow with hurt and anger.

"Yes," Gail managed.

"Then why do I have this feeling that you aren't real anymore? That you're trying hard to keep up a pretense that we still mean something to each other, but your heart isn't in it?"

Gail's panic rose into her throat. He stripped her bare with his black eyes, shattering her Monica facade and leaving her as exposed as the astonishing portrait in Alex Shepard's bedroom at Pinehaven. She felt Tom slipping away from her—from Monica.

"Please, Tom. Give me time."

"How much?" he asked impatiently.

"A few days. A week, at the most."

"Why? Why can't we work this out now?"

Gail stood speechless. It hurt her to see Tom suffering, even though she barely knew him. They were both victims, both she and Tom. But she had no answer for him and he stalked across the room to the front door. He paused there and looked at her. For a wrenching moment, Gail almost called him back. But he left, slamming the door behind him. Gail stood trembling with relief and regret.

She took her time wandering through the four rooms of Monica's apartment, absorbing the comfortable ambience of cherry-wood tables and deep-cushioned chairs. Past a set of French doors, Monica had her own small balcony. Gail stepped onto it, looking down at the pine tops that almost touched the rail.

Her own apartment back in Los Angeles had a single utilitarian window that looked onto a parking lot. It suddenly struck Gail that everything in her life had somehow become functional and work oriented. No man had ever had a key to her apartment. She closed her eyes.

The telephone rang, jarring Gail from her reverie. She went back inside and waited for the phone to ring again so she could find it. She spotted the chocolate-brown Trimline on a small cherry-wood desk near the bedroom door and picked up the receiver.

"Hello?"

"Don't you dare wear the beige knit dress with the handkerchief hem. I'm planning to get married in that."

"Monica!" Gail's heart jumped. "Where are you?"

"Safe—for now. Did you have any trouble finding my place?"

"No. I rode with Tom."

"Oh? Interesting." Monica made the word sound like a gross understatement. "How did you deal with that?"

"With a two-hour nap," Gail told her twin. "Look, this just is not working out, sister of mine. Tom is getting very upset with you." She couldn't bring herself to tell Monica that every time Tom kissed her, his displeasure rose a notch.

"We can worry about that later," Monica replied after a long pause. "Did he talk about Shadow?"

"He wants it over with, just like the rest of us."

Gail fidgeted at the desk as they talked. She pulled out the lap drawer, frowned at the clutter, then drew out the larger side drawer. The contents were in a mess.

"Monica, how neat are you?" she asked.

Another pause. "Why?"

"On a scale of one to ten, how neat?"

"Nine, on a bad day. Tom says he's going to give me lessons in the art of casual disarray. Why?"

"I think someone's been through your desk." And they weren't even as careful about it as whoever had gone through her suitcase at Pinehaven, Gail thought.

A knock interrupted their conversation. "Someone's at the door," she said, cupping her hand over the telephone and lowering her voice.

"I'll call you back when I can," Monica told her.

Before Gail could say anything else, Monica hung up. Gail slowly cradled the receiver, feeling as if a part of herself had been unplugged.

The knock came again. Still unnerved by Monica's call, she got up and opened the door. Alex stood filling the doorway, his hands in his pockets. While she gaped up at him, one hand came out holding the keys to Monica's Porsche.

"Joe and Dorie left your car in your slot," he said. "Adelaide picked them up and took them on over to her place." Alex looked past Gail into the apartment. "I didn't see Tom's car downstairs."

"He's already gone." Gail accepted the keys. "I begged out of going to Adelaide's this evening."

Alex remained standing there in the doorway, as if waiting for something. Gail couldn't think straight. They hadn't been alone together since they had left Pinehaven. Now she couldn't seem to pry her gaze off his chest to look him in the face.

"We have to talk, Monica," he said.

Gail reluctantly stepped back, her mouth as dry as bone, her mind in a daze. Alex moved past her and stopped in the middle of the living room, looking down at his feet. Gail closed the door, her heart pounding in her ears.

"Coffee?" she asked, to fill the awkwardness that seemed to hang in the air between them.

Alex nodded. Gail went into the tidy kitchenette off the dining alcove, and felt a rush of ice water through her veins; she didn't know where the coffee was. Alex had followed her from the living room. He leaned against the kitchen door frame, watching.

"Feel free to tell me it's none of my business," he said slowly, as if he knew he was about to step out of bounds, but had to do it, anyway. "Are you and Tom having serious problems?"

Gail spotted a Mr. Coffee machine. Very casually, trying to make it appear that she was only half paying attention to what she was doing, she began working her way through the cabinets.

"Why don't you ask Tom?" She tried to make it sound light, hoping he couldn't hear her heart thundering away. "He's your best friend." She found the mugs and placed two upon the counter.

Alex rubbed the back of his neck. "I don't know. I guess there are some things that men just don't feel comfortable talking to each other about," he admitted.

"But you feel comfortable discussing this with me!" *Where is the coffee?* Gail's nerves were stretched to the breaking point. He wouldn't take his eyes off her.

"To tell you the truth, Monica, I've never felt more uncomfortable around anyone in my life than I do right this minute." His dark eyes gazed directly into hers.

"I'm afraid I'm out of coffee," she said, unable to hide the tremor in her voice.

Alex kept staring at her. When he pushed himself away from the door frame and moved toward her, Gail's knees threatened to buckle. But instead of— what?—he reached past her to open a small cabinet door over the range hood.

Gail looked up at a stack of fluted filters and six unopened foil vacuum packs of coffee. Alex picked up the packs one at a time, then dropped them back onto the shelf and closed the door.

"Monica, I haven't said a word about your taking a week off at the worst possible time," he said, a hard edge creeping into his voice. "I figure you and Tom have your team tangled up, so I'll just let that subject ride for now. But I won't tolerate lying."

Gail stiffened, stung by his words. Everything about her was a lie, yet she was actually angered by his accusation.

"I forgot I had bought coffee. All right?" she said, her voice rising.

Her frustration began boiling to the surface, and she lifted her chin defiantly. How could the man stand there and reprimand her as if she were a four-year-old?

"To hell with the coffee," he said, waving a hand in a gesture of dismissal. "We'll all stop calling your stash the Tullahoma Coffee Warehouse. Okay? Just tell me one thing. Whatever took you away last week—will it interfere with your performance during Shadow's homestretch?"

"It most certainly will not," she declared crisply.

Alex moved back to the doorway, hands jammed into his pockets, broad shoulders hunched. Gail clenched her fists at her sides, angry with him for coming and scrutinizing her with his X-ray eyes.

She shouldn't have let him in.

Seeing her own anger mirrored in his eyes, Gail felt her emotions curdling into something she couldn't quite get a handle on. What could he do? Fire her? Kiss her? She held her breath, waiting for an ax to fall.

His hand came up to his eyes—a quick, testy movement, as if to swipe away cobwebs. Immediately Gail's mood changed from one of anger to one of concern. But she didn't dare go to him. Not as Monica, and certainly not as herself.

Alex tilted his head to one side, squinting at her with a tight expression that she couldn't read. The skin prickled on Gail's arms. She reminded herself that she was still a member of his team. Tomorrow she would walk through the gates at the Monarch testing facility and begin living her wildest dream.

"Is there anything at all you want to tell me, Monica?" he asked somberly.

Her mouth had turned to chalk. She couldn't have uttered a word if he had held a club over her. Was he seeing something? Perhaps sensing something?

Gail managed to shake her head, hoping her smile wasn't as garish as it felt. Alex pursed his lips, shrugged his shoulders, and turned to leave.

THE TIRES SQUEALED as Alex rounded the corner without slowing, gripping the steering wheel in two rigid fists. His white knuckles stood out in the moonlight. Damn! What was getting into him? Why did his feelings keep getting twisted out of shape when he was around Monica?

The blow on the head two days ago must have jangled his wits. Ever since then he had sensed a vulnerability that somehow was not Monica—therefore, it could not exist except in his imagination.

He told himself that, but he didn't believe it. Monica had returned with a gentle shyness that somehow spoke to the deepest, loneliest part of him. Alex had come away from their rambling walk in the woods with an overpowering awareness of her. It was almost as if he had never really known Monica before.

He slammed a fist against the steering wheel. Dammit, what about Tom?

"Shepard, you are such a jerk!" he muttered under his breath, braking sharply in front of Adelaide's house.

He counted the cars as he got out. The others were all there. Alex wished he had come early, instead of stopping by Monica's to deliver the keys. He could have saved himself a lot of grief.

Adelaide had left the front door open for latecomers. He let himself in and saluted the ragged cheer that his entrance brought from the living-room conversation pit, where Adelaide, Dorie and Joe were gathered around an enormous pizza.

Alex found Tom perched on a stool at the bar. From the looks of Tom, Alex gauged that he had already consumed a fair number of drinks.

"You'd better slow down there," Alex said, pouring himself a bourbon and soda. "We need to discuss the Shadow changes. Need I mention that you haven't exactly committed yourself to them yet?"

"What does that tell you?" Tom asked evenly, working on another highball.

Alex felt his temper flare. He tossed off the drink and poured himself another, trying to keep a lid on his cool. "You tell me," he said, more sharply than he had intended.

"All right." Tom spun around to glare at him point-blank. "I think it's irresponsible to make changes in the drone this late in the game."

"It's just a simple change, Tom."

"This late, there's no such animal." Tom reached across the bar and snatched the bottle from Alex's hand.

"You know what your problem is?" Alex waited for Tom to finish with the bottle, then snatched it back. "You're scared to be creative."

"Are you calling me a coward?" Tom's chest swelled righteously.

Alex eyed him over the rim of his plastic glass. The first drink was a warm puddle in the pit of his empty stomach. He hadn't eaten since breakfast, and the bourbon was already giving him a buzz. He glanced at Tom's flushed complexion and placed the bottle on the shelf under the bar.

"I want those changes, Tom," he said, in a tone that left no room for compromise.

Their eyes locked. Alex felt the hot flash of Tom's anger meet and match his own. Suddenly it was almost as if he and Tom were physically sparring with each other. Was it over something more than the design changes for the Shadow drone? Did it have to do with something—no, some*one*—who wasn't even in the room with them?

"Hey, you two," Adelaide said, leaving Dorie and Joe and marching over to the bar. "This is supposed to be a party. So knock it off."

Looking sullen, Tom swiveled around on the stool, turning his back upon Alex. Alex sighed. They had been through a lot together over the years. Alex knew their friendship would survive Shadow. He wasn't so sure either of them would survive Monica. It seemed that just when Shadow was coming together, his private life was falling apart. Well, he wouldn't have it. There was too much at stake, not just for himself, but for everyone. Alex lowered his drink to the bar, drew back his shoulders and set his jaw.

"I'm sorry, Adelaide," he said, watching Tom's hunched back. "But the party seems to be over."

Adelaide planted her fists upon her hips and looked exasperatedly at him, then at Tom. "What has gotten into you two?" she demanded.

With the help of the bourbon Alex managed a grim smile. "Shadow, Adelaide," he said. "Haven't you ever heard of pretest jitters?"

Tom audibly let out his breath and shook his head. Obviously making a point of not looking at Alex, he swung around on the stool, looped an arm over the bar, and retrieved the bottle from the shelf below.

Leaving Tom sitting there, Alex allowed Adelaide to lead him to the conversation pit. If downing a slice of pizza was to be the price of his exit visa, he was ready to get on with it.

GAIL PADDED across the room in her nightgown and opened the window nearest the bed. A cool breeze wafted in. She leaned on the windowsill, listening to the whispered soughing in the pines, trying to find a sense of peace within herself.

Exhausted, she gave up and turned back the bedspread. When she saw the sheets, she smiled wearily. They were forest green. Like the pine-scented breeze, they reminded her of Pinehaven.

She turned out the light and crawled into bed—Monica's bed. Mental fatigue had wrung the last ounce of energy from her body. Gail felt as if she were sinking into the mattress. She curled up and turned onto her left side. Her right side. Then stretched on her back.

Twenty minutes later she moaned in disgust. She was lying in Monica's bed—a bed that Monica quite possibly had shared with Tom Armstrong—and Alex Shepard was keeping her awake.

Alex frightened her, threatening her deception as he did. A part of her admired the bold, sometimes daring strides that he took in aeronautical technology. But another part of her was paralyzed by the force of his magnetism.

In less than three days she had come to desire Alex more than she had ever wanted any man. In a way she felt betrayed by her own weakness. How could she love a man who didn't even know she, Gail, existed?

Something in her deepest instincts told Gail that Alex was honest, decent and caring. But he also possessed a painting of Monica that could be nothing less than a visual representation of his most private fantasy.

Alex Shepard was, in short, a colossal contradiction.

An hour passed. Two. Three. Gail refused to look at the bedside clock as she tossed fitfully between the forest-green sheets that even in the darkness seemed to taunt her.

Finally, long after she had given up hope of sleeping that night, her eyelids began to grow heavy. Her feverish thoughts drifted—gradually disconnected. She sighed deeply, tugging the blankets higher under her chin.

She was already half-asleep when the bedroom door swung open.

CHAPTER SEVEN

SUDDENLY Gail was wide-awake again. She lay perfectly still, her heart pounding wildly, her gaze fixed on the dark doorway. Immobilized by fear, she could see nothing, hear nothing, and strained to see beyond the barely discernible door frame into the living room. Someone was in the apartment with her, and the closest thing she had to a weapon was her pillow.

She swallowed dryly. Slowly, cautiously, she raised herself onto one elbow, keeping her gaze riveted on the doorway. As the paralysis slowly receded, she had a crazy feeling that the moment to scream had passed.

The apartment felt incredibly isolated, as if the rest of the complex no longer existed. Through the open window she heard only the wind in the pines. She began to shiver uncontrollably.

She couldn't just lie there. She had to do something. Anything. If she didn't move, she would die of fright. Gail eased back the covers, suddenly conscious of her flimsy nightgown.

The telephone on the bedside table rang, shattering the silence. Gail cried out, then lunged for it. As she fumbled with the receiver, something in the living room crashed to the floor. She heard a muffled curse, a loud thump against a wall, frantic scurrying sounds, then the front door opening.

"Hello!" she gasped into the phone.

"Monica, I'm sorry to awaken you," Adelaide said. "Alex wanted me to call you about the early meeting he's ordered at the lab tomorrow, just in case..."

"Adelaide?" Gail couldn't seem to get out more than one word at a time.

"Monica, what's wrong?" Adelaide's voice had shifted tone almost in midsentence.

"Someone broke in t-to my apartment," Gail stammered. "I think the ringing telephone scared him off."

She crept out of bed, still trembling, still trying to see into the living room without letting go of the telephone. A shaft of light from the outside corridor shone through the open front door.

"Are you all right, Monica? Did he hurt you?"

"I'm okay—just scared silly. I didn't even see him."

"Are you sure the intruder is gone?"

"Yes. I think so. I'm going to call the police."

"No," Adelaide said firmly. "Alex will want the project's internal security force to handle this."

Gail didn't remember any mention of the Shadow project having an internal security force. "You're right," she said quickly, trying to cover herself. "Will you call them for me?"

"Yes, right after I call Alex. He lives closest to you. Just sit tight. We'll be right there."

The telephone clicked sharply in Gail's ear. She stood looking at the receiver, feeling abandoned, her heart still racing out of control.

It was over. Nothing had happened. She was still alone and afraid, but help was on its way. Gail straightened her shoulders and took a deep, calming breath. Moving stiffly, her muscles as taut as banjo strings, she forced herself to walk to the front door and lock it.

Less than ten minutes later, someone pounded on the door. Gail bolted from the couch to yank aside the kitchen chair she had wedged under the doorknob. Before she could reach the peephole, the fist struck again.

"Monica!"

She uttered a small cry at the sound of Alex's voice, her hands trembling as she worked the dead bolt. She finally got the door open and he rushed in, scooping her into his protective embrace. Gail clung to him, her cheeks pressed to his powerful chest, the sound of his raging heart echoing hers.

"You're all right," he said, stroking her hair. "Please, tell me you're all right."

Gail nodded. She felt him sigh. When he finally released her, they stood awkwardly apart. She saw that he had dressed hurriedly. His shirttail hung out, his cuffs flopped unbuttoned, and he wasn't wearing socks. He shoved his tousled hair off his forehead, his eyes still pinched with concern.

"Adelaide said someone broke in." Alex stepped back to examine the door locks.

"Someone *got* in," she corrected.

While she was telling him about the bedroom door easing open as she was nodding off to sleep, the elevator doors down the corridor whooshed open. Dorie trotted toward them, clad in a velour lounging suit and unlaced aerobics sneakers, with Adelaide following briskly in a neat wool coat dress and sensible shoes.

Gail waited for them. Alex looked toward the elevator, as if expecting someone else, then closed the door. Gail sank onto the couch before starting over— her voice steady now. When she finished, a brief silence settled over the group.

"Monica," Adelaide said, lowering herself onto the edge of the couch beside Gail. "Are you sure you weren't dreaming?"

Gail stared at her in disbelief. So did Alex. Dorie curled into an easy chair and toyed with her shoelaces.

"Dreams don't trip over tables and break things," Gail said, pointing out a broken vase that she had hastily placed on the end table after barricading the door.

"He must have been unfamiliar with the apartment," Adelaide observed.

"Or superklutzy," said Dorie.

"Or half-blind," Gail threw in. *Half-blind?* Something made her look at Alex. He was scowling at Adelaide.

"Where the hell's Tom?" he asked. "Didn't you call him?"

"I didn't see any point in it, Alex," Adelaide replied, smoothing the hem of her dress, her lips pursed. "We sent him home in a cab an hour or so after you left the party. He was in no condition to drive." She glanced at Gail. "Or to handle emergencies."

"Joe practically had to pour him into the cab," Dorie added. "I had no idea Tom drank like that."

"He doesn't," Alex said flatly.

He glanced at Gail and turned away. Hands jammed into his pockets, he wandered over to the French doors leading to the balcony, gazed at his reflection in the glass for a moment, then paced back to the center of the room.

"I'd like to use your phone, Monica," he said tersely. "I don't care what shape he's in. Tom ought to be here with you."

Gail motioned toward the bedroom. Alex stalked from the living room as she stared at him, puzzled. "It seems to me that Alex should be more concerned about having the police here than Tom," she murmured.

"He's just being practical about the police, Monica," Adelaide explained. "They're notoriously inept when it comes to investigating industrial espionage."

Espionage. Gail suddenly felt chin deep in her deception. She slid her hands under her thighs to hide their trembling.

"This could have been a common burglary attempt," she said, trying to sound convincing. "What makes you think it had anything to do with industrial espionage?"

Alex came back into the room, looking tense as she spoke. "Tom has his phone off the hook," he said irritably. "Now, what's this you were saying about espionage?"

"Adelaide thinks the break-in had something to do with Shadow, I gather," Gail told him, bewildered.

"But what would I have here that anyone would want?"

Alex studied Adelaide for a long moment, his arms folded across his chest as he rubbed his jaw. "Maybe you're right," he said finally and turned to Gail. "Monica, what did you do with that rough sketch I drew for you at Pinehaven, showing the alterations for Shadow?"

Gail had to think for a moment. Then she got up and went to the coat closet, returning with her purse. She opened it and slid her hand into an inside pocket.

"It's gone," she said.

They all stared at the purse. Alex clasped both hands behind his head and slowly raised both eyes to the ceiling. Ordinarily he would have burned the sketch. The blasted concussion had caused him to make an inexcusable security blunder.

"Okay, troops, what do we have here?" he inquired after a while. "Someone with a key—or a professional lock picker?"

"Tom and I have the only keys to this apartment," Gail told him, guessing wildly.

"So it was a pro," Alex went on. "Someone outside Shadow, who knew about the project. Someone who knew about the sketch, probably."

He looked at Dorie, Adelaide and Gail. Then back at Dorie. "An outsider with inside information," he said slowly, thinking aloud. "Dorie, where—exactly—did you meet Joe?"

"At my singles club." Dorie jumped indignantly to her feet. "And you can just forget about pinning this on Joe. Put it *out of your mind*." She made a slashing motion with both hands.

Alex shook his head. "Can't do that, Dorie. Not yet. I think it's about time we called the—"

"That's been taken care of," Adelaide cut in. "I called the authorities before we came over here."

"They're taking their own sweet time." Alex glanced at his wrist and realized he hadn't taken time to put on his watch.

"Gail told me she didn't see the intruder," Adelaide said. "So there can't be much she can tell them, anyway. They'll probably check downstairs first, to see if anyone suspicious was seen roaming around the parking lot."

Dorie remained standing, still puffed up with anger. Gail felt sorry for her. But then, remembering how her suitcase had been rifled that first night at Pinehaven, she had second thoughts. Dorie could be letting her feelings get in the way of good judgment. Maybe Joe Anderson was using her to get close to Shadow. It certainly was a possibility—one that deserved closer scrutiny. But not tonight.

"Look, it's late," Gail said placatingly. "There isn't much we can do about any of this tonight."

"Yes, there is," Alex said. "Adelaide, you'd better go brew some strong coffee and see how much of it you can get into Tom. I'll expect the entire Shadow team to be standing tall at the lab at six in the morning."

Adelaide rose from her chair with a nod. Taking Dorie in tow, she headed for the door.

"Adelaide . . . Dorie," Alex went on. The two women stopped at the door. "I'm counting on both of you."

"You won't be disappointed," Adelaide assured him. She nudged Dorie, who twisted her lips sulkily and nodded.

Alex looked strained as they left. Watching him rub the heels of both hands into his eyes, Gail began to see just how much the Shadow project meant to him. When he lowered his hands, his haunted expression filled her with dread. Then she knew that Shadow had crept into her blood as well, in the form of Alex Shepard.

She was still too upset by the phantom intruder to feel safe, and was grateful when Alex showed no inclination to leave. Even so, she couldn't overlook the perils involved in being alone with him in Monica's apartment. She had to balance her own needs against those of the job she had agreed to do.

"What do you say we take another shot at that cup of coffee we never got to yesterday afternoon, Monica?"

"The Tullahoma Coffee Warehouse is at your service," she said, jumping at his suggestion, and retreated toward the kitchen. At least this time, she thought with relief, she knew where everything was.

Gail had the Mr. Coffee machine primed and switched on before she realized Alex had followed her. He leaned against the door frame, arms folded and long legs loosely crossed. The way he was looking at her made Gail think of the portrait of Monica in the bedroom of his mountain retreat. The back of her neck flushed hotly, but she didn't dare ask him about the painting.

"Monica," he said, then paused, his lips tightening, as if he was about to broach a difficult subject. "You and Tom are obviously having serious problems."

Gail grabbed a dish towel and began polishing the spotless countertop. When she said nothing, Alex put a fist to his mouth and quietly cleared his throat.

"I guess what I'm trying to say is that I have no right to come between you and Tom, Monica. No right—and no desire to."

Gail stopped polishing and started wringing the towel in both hands. She could feel reality slipping away. Who was she? Gail Montgomery? Or Monica

Seabury? She looked up into his probing eyes and saw the deep feelings that he sought to deny. Gail was rocked with envy for Monica.

"I don't know what you're talking about," she said, twisting the towel into a hard knot.

"I think you do," he said. "I owe you an apology."

Gail swallowed with difficulty. The knot in the towel matched the one in her chest. She had felt so safe and secure when he swept her into his arms at the door, less than half an hour ago. Now she was floundering desperately, trying to keep her mind on an even keel in the rising tide of her emotions.

"Alex, I won't apologize for letting you hold me in your arms."

Gail was astounded by the sound of her own voice. She stood frozen, watching Alex straighten in slow motion, seeing his long arms and legs unfold as though in a dream. He stared at her, speechless, until she felt as if she were dissolving into the tile floor.

The Mr. Coffee belched. They both glanced at it. After that, she couldn't bring herself to look at him again. When he finally turned and walked out of the kitchen, Gail was appallingly aware that she had just taken Monica a giant step in the wrong direction.

ALEX WANDERED into the living room, feeling as if he had been struck in the gut with a wet sandbag. What was going on here, anyway? In a backhanded sort of way, Monica had just told him that she wanted him. Just a week ago, she wouldn't have given him the time of day—not in that sense.

Two weeks ago, you wouldn't have wanted her to, he thought. Two *days* ago, a tree had fallen on him. And when he awoke from that little disaster, his whole world had turned upside down.

Monica had changed. That was obvious enough. No wonder Tom had gotten bombed tonight. Alex dropped onto the couch, then sprang up immediately, too wired to sit still. This was not going to work. Tom was his best friend, and Monica was his...dream.

Alex shook his head, pacing the room, barely noticing the coffee aroma coming from the kitchen. He should have his mind on Shadow, but couldn't seem to think around Monica. Suddenly he was trapped between being either Tom's best man—or his worst enemy.

Monica's wine-colored attaché case sat closed but unlatched on the cherry-wood desk. He stopped and stroked the smooth leather, conscious of this new urge to touch things that belonged to her.

He flipped up the lid. An American Airlines ticket folder lay on top of a stack of papers. Alex peeked inside. Empty. Beneath it was a current issue of *Sci-*

ence Digest. He'd started to close the lid on the case, when he noticed the magazine's mailing label.

Alex leaned over for a better look. The label was addressed to a woman named Gail Montgomery, in care of Martindale Aircraft in Los Angeles.

He felt surprise loosen his jaw. He had a nodding acquaintance with Ab Calcutt, the head of Martindale's research division. But he'd had no idea that Monica knew anybody out there.

Alex fingered the ticket folder. Was that where she had taken off to last week? He glanced over his shoulder at the purse that Monica had left on the floor next to the easy chair.

Pieces began to come together—pieces that he didn't want to fit, forming a picture he didn't want to see. Monica's mysterious leave of absence, right in the middle of Shadow's homestretch. The airline ticket folder, along with evidence that she almost surely had had contact with someone at a leading aeronautical research firm. The missing sketch he had given her, supposedly stolen by an intruder whom, Monica claimed, she hadn't gotten a look at.

Listening to her moving around in the kitchen, Alex thought quickly. Maybe he was just being paranoid. Maybe he was just looking for a reason to not be dangerously in love with Monica Seabury. Or maybe he wanted to prove to himself that Monica hadn't been playing him and Tom for saps all these months. There would be time to sort out all that later.

For now, he peeled the mailing label carefully from the magazine and slipped it into his pocket. He intended to have his Dallas office check out this Gail Montgomery. He wanted to know who she was, before Monica observed another wind-tunnel test of Shadow. But he had a gut-wrenching feeling that the mysterious Miss M was going to turn out to be the worst possible creature: a Martindale engineer in the market for stolen Shadow research data.

Alex lowered the lid on the case and was standing across the room near the French doors when Monica stepped out of the kitchen carrying two mugs. He watched her come toward him, her body moving gracefully in the long, satin-trimmed robe, her bare feet treading soundlessly on the sculpted carpet.

With the lamplight in her auburn hair, she was as beautiful as he had painted her. She looked up at him as she handed him a mug. When he saw the quiver in her smile and the odd, shaky bravado in her eyes, Alex hated himself for wanting her in spite of everything.

CHAPTER EIGHT

GAIL WAS NOT READY to face the day as she awoke to her first morning on Monica's professional turf. It had been very late by the time Gail had convinced Alex to leave, assuring him the authorities would get around to her in their own good time. But they had never shown up and the break-in seemed less terrifying this morning. Indeed, there was a feeling of unreality about it, perhaps rooted in this bizarre dream in which she had become trapped.

She quickly showered and dressed and before long was on her way. In spite of the heavy cloud of anxiety, she enjoyed the twenty-minute drive to Monarch Space Center. She sped along the quiet streets beneath the canopies of tall trees that hovered like giant red and gold umbrellas. A gentle breeze stirred the dry leaves, sending them spiraling into the path of the Porsche as she passed through the parklike entrance to the center's grounds.

At the gate, a uniformed guard stepped from a small frame kiosk and checked Monica's identification card before raising the barrier and signaling her through. Gail felt only momentary relief as she drove on past three brick buildings and took a right curve into the parking lot. The real tests were yet to come.

She had arrived early, hoping for a chance to get her bearings in the sprawling facility before the other Shadow project team members showed up. But she felt grotesquely conspicuous as she entered through a set of wide glass doors and passed yet another security guard. Somehow she had a feeling that he watched her all the way to the elevator.

Concentrating on the directions she had memorized helped to squelch the butterflies in her stomach as Gail stepped off the elevator on the second floor and headed for the project offices to her right. Still, her hands shook so hard that she had difficulty inserting her plastic identification card into the coded door lock.

The lock disengaged, and she moved into the inner sanctum of the Shadow project. Any hopes she had harbored of having time to reconnoiter the premises alone were dashed immediately.

"Good morning, Monica," Alex said in a flat tone.

He stood in an open doorway at the end of a short corridor. His shirt sleeves were rolled up to the elbows, and his necktie rode at half-mast. He looked as if he had been hard at work for hours. Noting the dark circles under his eyes, Gail suspected that he hadn't been back to bed since leaving Monica's apartment.

"You should have left the bandage on another day or so," she said, blanching under his scowl. The angry laceration on his forehead from Friday's accident was only partly concealed by his tousled hair.

Alex stared mutely at the woman. He was afraid that if he spoke another word to her, he would lose his tenuous grip on the situation. Still feeling emotionally staggered, he simply turned on his heel and retreated into his office.

He went straight to his desk and pulled open the lap drawer. Once again he studied the mind-blowing likeness of Gail Montgomery. The photo had come in on his home fax machine, via his Dallas office, a bare ten minutes before Dick Brady showed up at his door. The next hour and a half had been extraordinary, to say the least.

According to Brady, last night's inquiries by Vince Aircraft Company of Dallas—inquiries Alex had instigated—had tipped the NSA officer's hand. So Brady had been forced to cut his losses and lay Gail's deception on the table. That had apparently been the easy part. The difficulty had been in convincing Alex that the man before him was not some kind of crackpot mental case.

Alex raked a hand through his hair. Hours after Brady had left, he was still rattled. The entire Shadow

project was balanced on that afternoon's two scheduled wind-tunnel tests. And on top of dropping the
Gail Montgomery bombshell, Brady had confirmed
what Alex had only begun to suspect: someone was
out to destroy the experimental drone.

Having brought the project of his lifetime to the
very brink of success, Alex was outraged by the possibility that Shadow's final triumph might yet slip
through his fingers. So, against his better judgment,
he had agreed to something that he already regretted. He would keep his mouth shut.

Brady had warned him that Gail was having difficulty keeping up her deception. If she learned that
Alex had uncovered her true identity, Brady feared
that her inexperience might lead her to let down her
guard just enough so that other Shadow project
members would become suspicious, as well.

Alex had placated himself with the knowledge that
he would have to sit on what he knew only until after
the wind-tunnel tests. And that it was the price he had
to pay to save Shadow. If he were totally honest with
himself, however, Alex would have to concede that he
had agreed to abide by Brady's gag order for far more
personal reasons. Reasons that rankled, burning
deeply into his pride.

He reached up and fingered the tender spot on his
head. Instead of reminding him of the blow that had
caused it, however, the bruised laceration triggered a

disconcerting recollection of Monica's—*Gail's*—delicate touch. Alex closed his eyes. He had made such a jackass of himself these past few days. She had played along with it while he practically threw himself at her.

The sense of humiliation bubbled up inside him, threatening to explode into anger. When this was all over, he was going straight back to Pinehaven to burn that damnable portrait. However much it had meant to Alex, the painting now seemed to mock him. He couldn't go on worshiping a figment of his imagination. Not when it turned on him the way this one had.

When Gail stepped into his office, Alex slammed the lap drawer of his desk, locked it, and pocketed the key. She smiled tensely, sensing that something else had happened overnight. Their gazes met with the same almost palpable force that continued to savage her inner calm. But now she detected something else in his cool expression: a pained sadness.

"Are you all right, Alex?"

"Fine," he said curtly.

Alex sat shuffling through the papers on his desk, glowering. As far as Gail could tell, he was making a point of ignoring her. She was anxiously trying to decide how to deal with that, when she heard the outer office door open behind her. Without turning, she recognized Adelaide's unmistakable footfall.

"RISE AND SHINE, chicken," Joe said, steering his pickup truck toward the curb outside Monarch Space Center's main gate.

Dorie shifted her head off his shoulder and looked around, yawning. "I can't believe I let you keep me up all night," she groaned.

"Me?" Joe grinned. "I thought it was your idea."

She sniffed demurely. But when he slid an arm around her shoulders, Dorie sighed and moved into his embrace. He was right—the night of lovemaking had been her idea. After leaving Monica's apartment in the wee hours, she had practically raced to Joe's place, livid over the accusations that had been leveled at him.

She still couldn't believe that Alex suspected Joe of breaking into Monica's apartment to steal the Shadow sketch. She kissed Joe now, as if to reaffirm to herself that her trust in him was still unblemished. Dorie tried not to think of the kiss or the night of passion as a form of vengeance on Alex Shepard for pointing the finger at Joe.

"Have you considered calling in sick this morning?" Joe murmured, nuzzling her ear.

"Lover boy, Alex wouldn't let me off today if I called in *dead*," she told him.

Joe straightened, hooking an arm over the steering wheel. "How come? What's so special about today?"

Dorie was tempted to tell him about the wind-tunnel tests. After all, Joe and everyone else in the area would know about them when the surrounding towns suffered an electrical brownout as the Tennessee Valley Authority diverted power to the enormous tunnel turbines.

The TVA usually granted the power diversion for Monarch's wind-tunnel tests only at night, when other customers would be least inconvenienced. But the urgency of the Shadow project had warranted the unusual daytime scheduling.

"You know I can't talk about what goes on in there," she said, as much to herself as Joe, nodding toward the security gate.

Joe sucked on his front teeth and stared into space, the playfulness suddenly gone from his expression. Dorie fidgeted. The highly classified nature of her work had always been a sticking point between them.

"I'm crazy about you, Dorie," he said after awhile.

"I love you, too," Dorie said wearily. Joe had a maddening habit of expressing his affection just when they were on the point of crossing swords.

"Prove it."

Dorie looked at him, startled. "What?"

"If you really love me, you won't keep secrets," he told her.

She sat very still, hoping he wasn't serious. When she realized that he wasn't kidding, Dorie momentarily grappled with indecision. Only belatedly did she awaken to the unfairness of his demand.

"If *you* really loved *me*," she said stiffly, "you wouldn't sit there playing games with my security clearance."

She grabbed her canvas purse from the floorboard and reached for the door handle. Joe's hand shot out and clamped around her forearm. When she started to pull away, his grip tightened.

"You're hurting me," she said bitingly.

He loosened his hold slightly. "I'm not asking you to commit treason, Dorie. For Pete's sake, what do you think I am? I just want to know that you trust me."

"I trust you enough to love you, Joe," she said, blinking back tears. "I'm really sorry if that isn't good enough for you."

Dorie jerked free, threw open the door and slid out of the truck cab. She slammed the door hard enough to bring the guard out of his kiosk fifty yards ahead.

"Dorie!"

She walked around the front of the truck to the driver's side, but didn't approach Joe's door. He rolled down the window and leaned out, glancing past her toward the kiosk and their one-man audience.

"I'm not trying to paint you into a corner, baby," he said, keeping his voice down. "I just don't like feeling shut out."

Dorie hugged her purse, watching his lips gradually deepen into a crooked, doghouse grin. Something inside her melted. Uttering a heavy sigh, she stalked to the door, stood on tiptoe, and planted a resounding kiss upon his cheek.

"I'll pick you up this evening," he called after her as Dorie turned and headed for the gate.

She waved over her shoulder, afraid to look back. She didn't want him to see her uncertainty. She would walk barefoot over hot coals for the man, and he darn well knew it. In the face of that, she couldn't understand why he still needed proof of her devotion.

At the gate she couldn't stand it any longer. She turned for one last parting look. Joe was still hanging out the truck window, watching her. She waved again and he blew her a kiss. And suddenly Dorie knew she would have to give him something—anything.

TOM WAS THE LAST of the Shadow team to arrive. He ambled into the offices, wearing white coveralls over his white shirt and necktie. He looked ragged around the edges, his face a sickly shade of hangover gray.

As he entered the room where the rest of the team had gathered around a large work table strewn with coffee cups, Gail saw his gaze flick toward her. She bit her lip, feeling his pain and confusion over the sudden and inexplicable rift that had arisen between him and "Monica." Gail desperately wanted to say or do something reassuring.

Ironically, she knew there were only two things she could do that would ease Tom's anguish. She could divulge her deception. Or she could surrender herself to the man whose baby Monica carried. And neither of these options could she consider.

Gail looked at him encouragingly, but saw Tom shift his gaze to Alex. Then, noticing that his colleague was studying her intently, Tom's eyes narrowed coldly.

"Cheer up, Thomas," Alex said solemnly, as if reading his friend's mind. "It's only a parlor trick."

"What are you talking about?" Tom moved closer to the table, but remained standing.

Alex chuckled humorlessly and rubbed his eyes. "Ask me that in a couple of days," he said. "I'll guarantee, it's a real knee slapper."

Tom folded his arms and frowned quizzically. "Alex, are you still having problems with that concussion?"

Alex raised a hand in a gesture of dismissal. "Forget it," he said. "Where have you been? I was about to send out a search party."

"I've been getting the technicians started on repositioning the brackets in the drone, to accommodate the shell game you're playing with the components," Tom told him, leaving no doubt in anyone's mind as to his opinion of the last-minute internal-design change.

Gail glanced across the table at Adelaide and Dorie. They were clearly expecting her to step in and smooth over the growing friction between the two engineers. Sensing that she was a major source of the undercurrent of conflict, she'd have preferred to stay out of it. But as Monica, she knew she had a job to do.

"Adelaide and Dorie have the revised design specifications," she added, concealing her uneasiness behind a brusque, businesslike tone. "They should have the new computer model ready, showing the proper placement of weight-balancing ballast, by the time your technicians are ready for it, Tom."

"Wonderful," Tom commented dryly. "Now, would someone please tell me why it's necessary to shift the microwave-sensor component package, when we're going to turn right around and fill the vacated space with *deadweight* that serves no purpose whatever?"

"Tom," she said patiently, "you know very well that the ballast has a purpose. We can't have the drone losing its aerodynamic integrity because of a shift in weight distribution."

Tom's brows rose slowly, and Gail realized at once that she was showing through her Monica facade. Unnerved, she shot a glance at Alex. He seemed to be concentrating on one of several computer printouts that he had brought to the meeting. A peculiar, barely perceptible smile teased the corners of his lips.

"Well, well," Tom said, his gaze jigging back and forth between Alex and Gail. "I see you've been receiving engineering lessons, Monica."

Gail wished that she had kept her mouth shut and let the two men work out their differences on their own.

"I'll be in the machine shop, Adelaide," Tom went on, without taking his eyes off Gail. "You'd best get a move on with that new computer model."

"Before you go," Alex said, "what about Colonel Bryant? Will he be here in time for the first test?"

"He's already here, hovering like a hawk," Tom said with visible displeasure. "The way he's behaving, you'd think Shadow was some kind of experimental weapon, instead of a harmless intelligence-gathering drone."

Alex stared back at Tom impassively. But Gail wondered if she was the only one in the room to notice Alex's cheek twitch. A tiny alarm went off in the back of her mind. She was pretty sure it had to do with the phrase *experimental weapon,* which Tom had tossed out like a test balloon.

Tom caught her staring intently at Alex and pivoted on one foot to stalk from the room. Adelaide sat still for a moment, as if waiting for invisible dust to settle. Then she rose sedately and followed Tom out, with Dorie trailing behind, looking preoccupied.

Elbows on the table, Alex propped his chin on his hands and stared grimly at the door. Gail saw him squeeze his eyes shut twice and guessed that he was still experiencing vision problems from the concussion. Recalling the stumbling intruder who had invaded Monica's apartment the previous night, she felt a sudden chill. Had the intruder been clumsy? Or— she cast a troubled glance at Alex—had he simply not been able to see where he was going?

"This is no way to run a railroad," Alex said abruptly. "Our team spirit seems to have gotten flushed down the toilet this past week."

Gail eased out of her chair. Being alone with Alex was too much like balancing on top of a land mine. She couldn't handle the deception of pretending she was Monica, while trying to convince herself that she wasn't falling in love with a man who would surely detest her when he discovered the truth.

"I need you, Monica."

Gail froze, almost afraid to ask, "For what?"

Alex produced a sealed manila envelope from beneath the printouts. He broke the seal beneath a red plastic Top Secret label, leafed through the contents and selected two sheets of blue paper, sliding them across to her.

"The design change that Tom is so dead set against is necessary to make room for this new component," he told her as she studied the computer graphic and the spec sheet. "This is for your eyes only, Monica. I need for you to make a copy of Adelaide's computer model as soon as she's finished and generate an additional model, using these specs."

"What the devil is this?" she asked, stalling, wondering if Monica knew how to generate a computer model. But then, why would he ask her to if she didn't?

"It's a signal-transmitting component that will be placed in the drone's forward compartment prior to the second wind-tunnel test this afternoon. The first test will establish the drone's ability to withstand stress. The second will check out the guidance system, the microwave sensors—and this." He tapped the graphic of the new component.

"All the outgoing signal equipment is located on top for satellite transmission," Gail observed, her scientific instincts suddenly going on point. "With this one placed in the belly, what kind of signal would you want to send . . . ?"

She choked as she realized what she'd asked, aware that she was on the verge of blundering into yet another revelation of her engineering expertise. She glanced up at Alex, again detecting that strange, vague half smile.

"Just do it, Monica," he said evenly.

Experimental weapon. The words were repeated over and over in her head. But the two sheets of paper in front of her contained only the bare minimum of data that she would need to produce the computer model.

"Does Tom know about this?" she asked.

"Not yet." Alex stared pensively toward the door. "And under the circumstances, I have doubts about even bothering to tell him about the rest of it."

"The rest of it?"

Alex held up the manila envelope, which presumably contained the full story of the mysterious new component. Gail studied the graphic sheet again and decided that the component could conceivably turn the drone into an offensive weapon.

Could. That didn't mean that it did. But *if* it did, Alex's bland expression told her that he wasn't at all bothered by the prospect. For the second time in minutes, Gail felt a chill.

HARD AT WORK at Monica's computer terminal, Gail absently glanced up at the wall clock and blinked. *One-fifteen.* She had worked straight through lunch without realizing it. The first wind-tunnel test was scheduled to take place in less than fifteen minutes.

She quickly stored the work she had completed and rushed out of Monica's office to the space that Adelaide and Dorie shared two doors down the corridor. They were gone.

A tiny ice cube of panic fell onto the floor of her stomach and began to grow. With her sketchy grasp of maps, Gail hadn't been able to memorize the entire layout of Monarch Space Center. She had intended to walk to the test site with Adelaide. There was no way she could find it on her own in just fifteen minutes.

"Why aren't you already at the tunnel, Monica?"

Gail whirled around as Alex barged from his office, the hem of an unbuttoned white lab coat kiting behind him. He looked harried.

"I lost track of the time," she said.

"Well, saddle up. You can ride over with me." He put both hands to his head, as if trying to remember something. "If I can just get my act together."

Alex disappeared back into his office. Gail was torn between dashing out the door and trusting her luck to find the test site on her own or waiting for him. The longer she had worked on the computer model, the more the new mystery matched the pattern of a laser weapon of some sort.

She still found it hard to believe that her judgment of Alex Shepard's character could be so far off base. But she didn't want to be close to him until she'd had more time to think. At the moment, however, she had no choice.

He charged from his office again. Gail trotted after him to the elevator, and barely a minute later, they climbed into an electric cart in the parking lot.

"Hang on," he ordered. "If we're late, the TVA won't divert the power to Monarch for the test, and Colonel Bryant will go into meltdown."

Gail couldn't find a handhold anywhere. Alex stomped on the small accelerator pedal, and the cart nearly bucked from under her. Just as she did a nosedive off the narrow bench seat, Gail felt his arm snake around her waist and scoop her back on board.

He swerved the cart around a pavement barrier, jumped it onto a sidewalk and floored the accelerator.

"You're a very creative driver," she commented.

"Yeah. But I'm a lousy putter," he said, straight-faced. "Can't finish eighteen holes under par to save my life."

Gail closed her eyes, unable to watch their pell-mell progress through suddenly wide-eyed foot traffic. Alex didn't let go of her, and despite her qualms about being pressed against him, she didn't want him to. She grabbed a handful of his lab coat and hung on.

The cart whined to a stop in front of the wind-tunnel annex. Alex vaulted over Gail's legs, swept her unceremoniously off the vinyl seat, and clamped a big hand around her forearm. Together they sprinted into the building.

Monarch's enormous wind tunnel was similar to the one Martindale used at Sunnyvale in California. Gail instantly felt at home in the cavernous, fifty-thousand-square-foot building. As she and Alex slowed to a rapid walk, she glanced around at the scattered workmen.

To her surprise, Gail spotted Howard Eastman on the fringe of one of several groups clustered near the tunnel observation points. She quickly looked away, avoiding eye contact with the Defense Department officer. But she couldn't help feeling more secure, just knowing he was nearby.

Gail's attention skipped to another group, settling on a stocky man standing near the front. She did a double take and would have stopped cold if Alex hadn't dragged her along in his headlong rush toward the control center. She looked back, searching for the face she had never expected to see again, particularly on these premises.

The crooked eye was unmistakable. It was the same man who had been changing a tire on the highway near Pinehaven last Friday. She was too far away to read the name on his Visitor's identification tag. When he saw her looking at him, he quickly moved to the back of the group and out of sight.

His sudden furtive movement sent Gail's mind reeling. Who was he, and what was he doing there? She glanced toward Eastman, but once again quickly averted her gaze. She dared not talk to anyone about the crooked-eyed visitor, for fear of giving herself away.

"I hope you have all your fingers and toes crossed," Alex murmured as they approached the control center.

A wall of air force uniforms faced them. Tom and Adelaide stood near the official military observation party, looking outrageously civilian in their floppy lab coats. Tom coolly turned away. Had he noticed that Alex's fist still gripped Gail's arm? She discreetly extricated herself and went to stand near Tom.

"It's about time, Shepard," an officer snapped, breaking away from the pack of blue uniforms. Gray-haired and ramrod straight, he wore an impressive block of campaign ribbons on his barrel chest.

"I'm *in* time, Colonel Bryant," Alex shot back. "That's all that counts."

The two men glared at each other, Bryant's nose quivering as if he smelled something foul. Alex stared at the officer's pompous expression, then slowly smiled and shook his head, as if he couldn't quite believe what he was seeing.

"Blowers powering up," Tom announced into the silence.

Alex appeared to jerk free of Bryant's piercing gaze and stepped over to the controls as the sound of the wind tunnel's huge fan assembly thrummed through the building. Beyond the viewing window, the sleek Shadow drone perched atop its pedestal inside the tunnel. Alex quickly checked the monitors that relayed information.

Gail felt her excitement skyrocket as the wind velocity rose inside the tunnel, heading for a peak of over three thousand miles per hour. She took a step toward Alex, whose gaze darted continuously from the drone to the controls and the monitors.

Barely seconds into the test, the drone model suddenly listed to one side, visibly vibrating under wind speeds already exceeding the highest hurricane force ever recorded. Gail watched Alex's hands dance frantically over the controls, his face mirroring her own alarm.

"Abort," he said sharply.

"Power down!" Tom shouted.

The thrum of the monstrous turbines gradually subsided. As the wind dropped within the tunnel, the Shadow model ceased its tortured shuddering and hung motionless, nose down, like a mammoth dragonfly impaled on a rose thorn.

For a moment the scattered observation groups simply stared at the disabled model. Then, as if someone had thrown a switch, a babble of voices erupted, Colonel Bryant's rising above the others.

"Shepard, that is the most pathetic, incompetent demonstration I have ever witnessed!"

Alex drew his hands away from the controls and looked past Gail at Tom, clearly ignoring Bryant's comment. The test failure appeared to have stymied both engineers and Gail saw them shake their heads in disbelief.

"Did you hear me, Shepard?" Bryant bellowed.

Alex turned toward the red-faced officer. "I don't happen to agree with you, Colonel," he said through his teeth. "But I expect half of Franklin County *heard* you."

Bryant turned a deeper shade of rage red. Gail noticed that when he spoke again, his voice was lower, but had lost none of its threatening tone.

"I want to know precisely what went wrong in there," Bryant said, jabbing a finger toward the drone.

"Well, join the club," Alex shot back.

Their exchange was rapidly escalating toward a head-on collision of wills. Gail realized she couldn't just stand by and allow the test disaster to spread beyond the controlled confines of the wind tunnel.

"Colonel Bryant," she said, forcing calmness into her voice, "I'm sure you're aware that Dr. Shepard will require some time to evaluate the situation before the problem can be pinpointed.''

Bryant looked down at her with open contempt. "*Time* is in short supply, sweetie," he said acidly.

Gail bristled, feeling her cheeks burn as if he had slapped her. "You obviously do not understand the complexities involved in this test, *sweetie,*" she retorted.

"Monica!"

Gail flinched at the sound of Tom's voice. Now it was the colonel's turn to look slapped. She knew she had overstepped the limits of her role, but she had a low tolerance of condescension. Especially coming from a brass blowhard who obviously liked to throw his weight around.

She began to waver under the laserlike thrust of Bryant's wrathful gaze. Gail was on the verge of apologizing, when she felt a hand lightly press the small of her back, and remembered that she was standing directly in front of Alex. His discreet gesture of support sent a thrill up her spine.

"Colonel Bryant, just for the sake of argument, why don't we all pretend we're adults for a moment?" she suggested, donning a plastic smile, straining to lighten a situation that had become as unstable as old dynamite. "How about telling us where the Shadow project stands right now, as far as the air force is concerned?"

"It stands in deep—" Bryant chopped off the sentence, appeared to regroup, and started again. "Unless the test can be successfully completed within thirty-six hours—*Miz*—I'll have no choice but to recommend cancellation of the entire program."

"Cancel?" Gail caught Tom's grim expression and could only imagine what kind of look the colonel's ultimatum had triggered on Alex's face. "After it's come this far?"

"Just how far *has* it come?" Bryant asked, edging back toward sarcasm. "That's what you people were supposed to demonstrate this afternoon."

"Colonel Bryant," Tom said, moving to Gail's side. "The TVA won't let us reschedule a test on such short notice, even if we manage to find and solve the technical problem that fast."

"Another research group has booked a test for tomorrow night," Bryant told him, visibly unwilling to give an inch. "Bump them, and use that time yourself."

"We don't have that authority!" Tom protested.

"Then I suggest that you find someone who does, Armstrong," Bryant said.

Gail took one look at the blood rising into Tom's face, and hastily maneuvered the confrontation toward a temporary cease-fire.

"Thirty-six hours it is, Colonel Bryant," she agreed. "And since time is in such short supply, as you say, I'm sure you'll want to leave us to our work now."

The air force officer scowled, clearly torn between acknowledging Gail's logic and exercising his self-appointed right to remain in the control center. For the sake of the imperiled Shadow project, Gail was about to suggest that Adelaide go along to answer any questions the colonel might have, when Alex spoke up.

"Tom, why don't you take the colonel back to the office complex and show him the computer simulation?" Alex proposed. "It'll give him an idea of the complexities we're up against here."

Tom looked as surprised as Gail felt. Their eyes met fleetingly. In that instant, she sensed exactly what Tom was thinking and why: Alex was trying to get rid of him because of Monica. Under the circumstances that was an absurd idea. But Gail was beginning to accept absurdity as a way of life.

Colonel Bryant turned to lead his entourage from the building. Gail watched Adelaide attach herself to the group, her distinct gait somehow looking even more military than theirs.

"What are you trying to pull, Alex?" Tom asked in an angry undertone, placing a possessive hand on Gail's shoulder.

"You can reason with that arrogant jerk," Alex said. "I'd have my hands on his throat before we got out of the parking lot. Stroke his brass-plated back-side, and maybe he'll help us get Shadow resched-uled into that test period tomorrow night."

"Alex is right, Tom," Gail agreed, squeezing Tom's hand with all the feeling she could muster in Monica.

Tom backed away two paces, both hands fisted at his sides, looking like a man staring betrayal in the face. Before Gail could say anything more, he stalked from the control center. Alex stared after him long after he was gone.

"Alex, was that necessary?" Gail knew it was part question, part accusation. As project test manager, Tom could be instrumental in determining the cause of the wind-tunnel failure.

"Right this minute he's too biased to think straight."

Gail hugged herself defensively, expecting Alex to blame her for splitting up what should have been a team effort. She soon found she was wrong.

"Tom's been dead set against the last-minute de-sign changes from the beginning," Alex said. "He'll start out trying to prove they caused the failure, in-stead of keeping an open mind."

"So what do you think is to blame?" Gail asked.

"I haven't the foggiest." Alex started toward the wind tunnel. "But I'm damn well going to find out."

The building had emptied of all but the technicians involved in operating the complex test equipment. Alex was oblivious even to them as he charged toward the tunnel, head down, his mind seething. He almost wished the fault would turn out to be in the late design changes. But even Tom would see the futility in trying to place blame there, if he could just manage to take Monica out of the equation.

"Alex!"

Gail ran to catch up. She had to grab his sleeve to get his attention. "Alex, did you notice that one of the monitors has gone dead?"

Alex looked back toward the control center. His expression shifted from worried to puzzled. He tilted his head to one side, staring straight at Gail without appearing to see her.

"You don't say," he said, dragging the words out in a slow Texas drawl.

Gail studied the sudden, predatory alertness in his eyes. With a tremor of excitement, she knew this was what she had dreamed about—sharing the process of discovery with Dr. Alex Shepard.

"Okay, you've put us onto a scent," he said. "Let's go see if that dog will hunt."

Only when he turned back toward the wind tunnel did Gail realize she was still clutching his sleeve.

CHAPTER NINE

ALEX CIRCLED the Shadow drone, visually examining the model from all angles. His strong, suntanned features had lost all expression and his eyes had widened, as if he had opened himself to all possibilities.

Gail stood to one side and watched, feeling like a green student observing a wise professor. He whistled softly through his teeth, totally focused on the model. He strolled around the drone again, hands folded behind his back, teasing her anticipation to almost sensual heights.

Finally Alex stopped and put his hands on the underside of the model, where a double bracket secured it. Still whisper-whistling, he motioned her closer.

"The bolt on this bracket is gone." He pointing out where the bracket had been wrenched from its base during the aborted test, allowing the model to list sharply to one side.

"Someone neglected to tighten it down?" Gail had taken part in numerous wind-tunnel tests at Sunnyvale and had never seen that happen.

"Nope. Tom personally supervises the anchoring. This bracket is the last thing that should have failed."

"But it did."

"Spectacularly." Alex turned and strolled off toward the far end of the long wind tunnel, his hands in his lab-coat pockets. He kept his head down, as if thinking.

Near a heavy grating at the end of the tunnel, he stopped and toed something with his shoe. Then he bent and picked up a small object, turning it over and over in his hands as he walked slowly back toward Gail.

Alex took her hand in his, with an unconscious gentleness that drew her gaze upward. He frowned softly at her, his hand tightening around hers, a vein in his forehead pulsing near the bruised laceration. Gail was tempted to reach up and brush his hair from the healing wound. As that thought ran through her mind, she felt something hard and cold press into her palm.

"One missing bolt," he said as she looked down at the misshapen chunk of metal. "It's flattened on one side where the wind slammed it into the grate back there. But as you can see, the threads aren't stripped on its good side."

Gail stared at it dumbly, her mind thrown out of gear by the feel of his hand still cupping hers. Then the significance of what he was saying finally struck home.

"The bolt wasn't wrenched from the bracket? It worked itself free?"

"Vibration could do that, if it wasn't properly tightened."

"But Tom would have made sure that it was," she pointed out.

Alex nodded and dropped her hand. "That probably tells us something." He turned back to the sting.

"Such as?"

"Let's not start analyzing until we have all the data." He got a hold on the drone model and turned it around just far enough to expose the wiring collar at the top. "So, now let's see if unpleasant surprises *always* come in twos."

Gail thought his last remark sounded oddly snide, but let her mind skip past that impression as he worked the wiring up and out.

Alex grunted sharply at the sight of melted insulation. "Is anybody watching?" he murmured under his breath.

Gail glanced back toward the observation points. "Just a handful of fellow white coats."

"Good." He whipped a small adjustable-beam flashlight from his pocket, and aimed it down the hole he had exposed. "Do you see what I'm seeing?"

Gail pressed up so close that she could smell the faint residue of his early-morning after-shave lotion. He raised one arm so she could move still closer. Gail reached up and tilted the flashlight beam to her angle.

"A wiring short," she said, examining the scorched interior. Several wires had damaged insulation, and one had been burned clear through. "That explains the dead monitor in the control center."

"Come on, Monica," he said, coaxing. "What else do we see?"

She glanced at his face, just inches above hers, and saw a mixture of tension, anger and excitement. She took another look.

"The inside is scorched—a lot," she said. "It looks more like it's sustained a small explosion than a simple short."

"Match that up with the improperly secured bracket, and what do we have?"

Gail backed up a step, suddenly put on guard by his barrage of questions. "You're the engineer," she said, reluctantly shelving her own conclusions. "You tell me."

Alex pocketed the flashlight and dug a hand into his pants pocket, eyeing her the way a cat watches a caged bird. Gail couldn't see past that hooded gaze, but had an uncomfortable feeling that he was looking right down into her very soul.

"You remember the tests we ran some time ago, using small plastic explosives charges, when we were perfecting the self-destruct mechanism?" he asked, producing a red-handled Swiss army knife.

Gail nodded—another lie, she thought.

"Don't you think the scorch pattern inside bears a striking resemblance to the ones we produced in the lab?" he asked.

His leading questions were making her jumpy. So was standing close to him. She moved a few paces away, trying to clear her mind and her emotions.

"You're making this sound like sabotage, Alex."

"Am I?"

"Stop playing games," she told him, speaking more sharply than she had intended.

He lowered his head as if to peer at her over the tops of non-existent glasses, smiling sardonically. "That gets my vote," he said flatly.

"How could a saboteur detonate an explosive device in here without being seen?" she inquired, wrestling with an almost visceral feeling that Alex was somehow mocking her.

"With a remote-control detonator, just like the one we used in the lab," he said. "He probably wouldn't even have to have been inside the building."

The bolt in Gail's hand suddenly felt heavy. She fingered the chunk of cold steel and the cold spread up her arm and into her chest.

Detonator. Plastic explosives. The words made a connection with the other phrase that had hung like an evil shadow in the back of her mind all morning: *experimental weapon.*

"This is beginning to scare the willies out of me," she said.

"Me, too."

In an odd sort of way, his surprising admission made Gail feel closer to Alex. This was something she could openly share with him. Alone and isolated in her deception, her need to reach out to Alex was becoming as powerful as a desert thirst.

Alex opened the wire-stripping blade on his pocket-knife and went to work on the severed wire they had discovered. As he deftly repaired it and checked the others, he kept glancing at his watch.

"We still have a half hour," he said, when he was finished.

"Until what?" Gail asked.

"The second wind-tunnel test." He turned to scan the faces of half a dozen technicians who had wandered over to the observation points outside the tunnel. "We were scheduled for two this afternoon."

"Surely you don't mean to go through with the second one now?"

Alex signaled to one of the technicians and smiled at her. "Monica, after the dressing-down you gave Colonel Bryant following the test failure, there's no way I'm going to place all my bets on tomorrow night's test—assuming we can even get it scheduled. Besides, the TVA is expecting those turbines to power up again in—'' he checked his watch ''—exactly thirty-two minutes. Why disappoint them?''

Gail watched in astonishment as the burly technician entered the tunnel. She had assumed that the second test of the afternoon had been canceled after the failure of the first. After all, wind-tunnel tests required extensive planning and preparation. Surely Alex knew better than to risk severely damaging the drone with what now amounted to a snap test.

''Walt, get this bracket secured.'' Alex directed the technician's attention to the bracket from which the bolt had worked free. ''When you tighten it down, I want to see two men on a torque wrench.''

''You've got it,'' Walt assured him.

''This is crazy!'' Gail declared, following Alex out of the tunnel.

''No. It's daring, Monica. There's a difference.''

Back at the control center, Gail watched a squad of technicians swarm around the drone model as Alex checked the monitors. Nervous, she picked up a clipboard containing a pretest checklist. Caught up in the adrenaline surge of the pressure situation, she quickly entered the correct time in the control center's digital countdown clock.

''I'd better get Tom back over here,'' she said.

"We'll do just fine without him." Alex had stopped checking the monitors. His gaze had fixed on the countdown clock.

Gail could have kicked herself. She had set the blasted clock without thinking. Drawing upon her test experience at Sunnyvale, she knew how much had to be done in the short amount of time remaining. She couldn't just stand around and play dumb.

Alex had no idea how long he remained mesmerized by the countdown clock. When he'd seen Gail setting it, something inside him had taken a giant leap forward. Her setting the clock was such a simple thing, on the surface. But deep down, the act drew an imaginary line in sand. On one side stood Monica Seabury. On this side—next to Alex—stood Gail Montgomery.

For the first time since Dick Brady had sat on his couch and blown Gail's cover, Alex didn't feel emotionally ravaged by the discovery. He began to see Gail for the intelligent, courageous woman she was.

Sure she was frightened. But she'd had the strength to hold her course, even after the intruder had broken into Monica's apartment last night.

"I'll read off the checklist," Gail said, as technicians began taking up positions in the control center. Even Monica could do that, she decided. Relieved that he hadn't said anything about the countdown clock, Gail began working her way down the checklist, picking up speed as the test crew called out responses.

When Walt signaled that the brackets had been secured, Alex dashed back into the tunnel to check them himself before allowing the wind-tunnel door to be closed and sealed. Looking uneasy, Walt accompanied Alex back to the control center and came over to where Gail was standing.

"Monica," he said, in a half whisper. "Where the devil is Tom? He'll have kittens if this test is carried out without him."

"I heard that, Walt," Alex said from the control console. "You let me worry about Tom. For the next fifteen minutes you've been promoted to test coordinator. Get over here and earn your keep."

The countdown clock blipped off the final ninety seconds in slow motion as Gail watched. She was not aware that she had drifted closer to the control console until her shoulder brushed Alex's arm. She felt his biceps—a steely knot beneath the sleeve of his lab coat.

"Good luck," she murmured, swallowing dryly.

"Thanks," he whispered, his voice sounding tight with tension.

"Blowers powering up," Walt called.

Gail held her breath, watching the tunnel's wind-velocity monitor. As the reading approached the point where the earlier test had gone awry, Alex leaned into her, applying body language to the drone model. She leaned back. Together they mentally piloted the drone past the spot marked by its previous disaster.

"Go for it, angel," Alex said as the wind speed continued to climb.

The drone model remained steady on its perch, its high-tech alloy surface withstanding the stress of the tremendous wind pressure. The wind speed reached its peak, and Gail quickly scanned the monitors that registered and recorded the test data. Her cheeks began aching from her sustained grin.

"Powering down," Walt said minutes later.

All eyes in the control center remained fixed on the drone until the turbines gradually slowed to a stop. A ragged cheer erupted from the technicians.

"Beautiful!" Alex shouted, exultant.

Gail let out a triumphant whoop and threw her arms around his neck as Alex turned to embrace her. He lifted her off the floor, squeezing the air from her lungs, laughing as he spun her around in a dizzy circle.

She planted a kiss upon his flushed cheek, her head swimming euphorically. They clung together, spontaneously sharing the moment.

Alex suddenly seemed to realize what he was doing and released her. Gail's lithe body slid down his long frame. Her feet touched the floor, but her mind remained stranded somewhere in the stratosphere.

For a moment it had seemed that they had become one entity—one being. Now she was having trouble regaining her footing—in every sense.

Feeling disoriented, seconds passed before Gail noticed the techs staring at her with amusement. Embarrassed, she glanced at Alex. He looked as if he had just swallowed something enormous.

"Nice going, Monica," Walt said, somehow combining a smile with a studious frown.

Monica. Gail felt the blood drain from her face. She knew she had just made a public spectacle of herself. But she felt oddly detached, as if it really had been Monica and not Gail who had thrown herself into Alex Shepard's embrace. As far as Alex was concerned, she realized, that was exactly what had happened.

"Walt, I want to secure the drone," Alex said, his voice sounding uncertain and hoarse.

"Might as well leave it there," Walt replied, "until you find out if you're scheduled for another test tomorrow night."

Alex pursed his lips, considering his options, then nodded. "We'll just check it over before we leave." He nodded toward Gail. "Then I want a security guard on it until the test. Nobody...*nobody* is to go near it until then. Understood?"

"Consider it done," Walt assured him.

Alex took Gail's elbow and steered her toward the tunnel. Again she watched him circle the model. This time, however, he was smiling confidently, his tanned face still flushed with excitement. As he traced a finger lovingly along Shadow's swept wing, Gail felt a fiery wave of envy for the drone.

"Did you finish the computer model for the new component package?" he asked.

Gail started, trying to focus on his question. "Almost."

"Good. We might as well go ahead and remove the ballast, then," Alex said, preparing to detach a panel from the side of the drone.

"Why not let the technicians do that?" Gail asked, anxious to get back to the main building, where she could shut herself up in Monica's office. Ever since letting herself get carried away in the excitement of the moment in the control center, she had felt as if a part of her were drowning in the turbulent aura surrounding Alex. "Better yet, let Tom do it."

"Tom's already steamed at me," he said. "You know that. When it comes to the subject of ballast, I'd just as soon leave him out of it."

Alex freed the panel and placed it on the floor. Gail got her first look at the drone's interior, which she had previously seen only in diagrams and computer models.

"Why did you bother with the ballast?" she wanted to know, as he loosened more metal plates. "Why didn't you just install the new component package when the microwave sensors were moved out of the way this morning?"

"Because the air force won't release the device to us until we demonstrate a workable drone concept—which we hadn't done until this second test."

Gail stared at the back of his head, struck by a fresh current of doubt. His tawny hair undulated in a natural wave toward the collar of his lab coat. She wanted so very much to touch his hair, to feel again its softness between her fingers. At the same time, she had an increasingly powerful urge to run away from him, because of the hideous things she was thinking.

She had to know. She mustered her courage and asked, "Alex, is the new signaling device some kind of—weapon?"

Gail had to force out the last word. His hands paused in their work on the ballast, his broad shoulders rising slightly as he took a deep breath. She prayed for a denial.

Her heart sank when he resumed work without answering. She took his silence to be the most shameful kind of confirmation and for a moment almost wished he had lied to her. Then Gail thought of Monica carrying Tom's unborn child and realized she would never be satisfied with anything less than the truth about the Shadow project. If Alex was really masterminding a killing machine, she could not remain a part of the project. She doubted if even her feelings for Alex could survive such a dark reality.

Alex had almost finished removing the ballast. Gail leaned over, pinching her lips together, and took a closer look at the drone's interior. She regretted having helped with the wind-tunnel test. Had she known the Shadow project might involve weaponry, she never would have agreed to step into this mess.

Gail studied the drone's tightly packed, supersecret components, still not wanting to believe the worst of Alex. Matching up what she could see with the computer model she had worked on earlier in the day, she spotted the microwave sensor unit that Tom had so reluctantly shifted that morning. Next she noticed the heat-resistant shield that Tom had installed to insulate the sensor from the drone's engine heat.

She saw a scratch on the insulating panel's forward surface and was reaching toward it, when Alex suddenly grabbed her hand and jerked it away. His abrupt movement nearly knocked her off balance. His hand welded to her wrist, Alex froze Gail with a look of white-lipped fury.

CHAPTER TEN

"SON OF A *BISCUIT!*" Alex snapped. "What next?"

Gail staggered backward, slipped, and would have fallen if he hadn't spun around and caught her. She squirmed in his grasp. When he realized she was frightened, Alex released her and raised both hands placatingly.

"Sorry," he said. "I didn't mean to scare the socks off you. But this is crazy."

"What?" Gail rubbed her wrist, where his fingers had left red marks. Her heart leaped in her chest. One more minute of this insanity, she thought, and she would be a basket case.

"This." Alex wedged three fingers around the back end of the sensor package, and with the help of a screwdriver worked loose a dome-shaped metal unit. He glared at it briefly, then held it out to Gail. "Counterfeit."

"How can you tell?" she asked, still shaken.

"For one thing, it's a much lighter weight than it should be."

"Oh. You spotted that before you removed it, did you?"

"Be serious, Monica." Alex took back the metal part and ran a finger over the smooth, domed end. "Actually, what I spotted was this shape. We changed the design to a flat configuration a couple of months ago. This was molded after the old version."

Gail slipped her hands into her lab-coat pockets to hide their trembling, and grazed her knuckles on a sharp edge of the disfigured bolt. She pulled it out and looked at it, feeling as if she were missing a connection somewhere.

"Alex, this doesn't make any sense at all," she said, holding up the bolt. "Why would someone go to all the trouble to sabotage the wiring, when the resulting test failure was bound to draw attention to that counterfeit part?"

"You have a point." Alex snatched the bolt from her and pocketed it along with the counterfeit part.

Frowning, deep in thought, he picked up the drone model's exterior panel and began carefully fitting it back into place. Gail's skin prickled. She had an eerie feeling that they were being watched. But when she looked past Alex to the observation points, she found them all empty.

"You know, I've had it up to here with counterfeits," Alex said testily, pausing to draw a line across his creased forehead with the screwdriver handle.

"What are you going to do about it?" Gail dragged her gaze uneasily from the observation points.

Alex looked over his shoulder at her, his lips parted, plainly on the verge of speaking. His gaze bored into her, as if he were trying to tell her something without putting it into words. Then his jaw slid slowly to one side. Gail had a distinct impression that, for some reason, he had changed his mind.

"I'm not sure," he said with a troubled shake of his head. "Right now, the critical question is, who has the original?"

"And who has the remote control device that set off the explosives charge?" she inquired.

"Are they even the same people?" he added.

Suddenly Gail remembered the crooked-eyed man from the highway outside Pinehaven, whom she had seen among the observers of the failed wind-tunnel test. It seemed wherever she saw this man, bad things happened. First the falling tree, then the sabotaged Shadow test. Gail recalled the break-in at Monica's apartment. She'd been right about the stumbling intruder; he had been visually impaired. But she'd suspected the wrong man. Her gaze shot as if drawn by a magnet to the bruised laceration on Alex's forehead. Had the wound been caused by an accident?

Gail couldn't seem to get enough air into her lungs. Confused and frightened, she realized she had ventured much too far out from the orderly environment of her own scientific world. Lured here by Monica, and by the prospect of working briefly alongside Dr. Alex Shepard, now she felt as though she was drowning. She knew she was just having an anxiety attack, and that she would be able to breathe just fine if she could just calm her trembling. But she couldn't.

As if reading her thoughts, Alex pulled her protectively to him. For just a moment, standing there enveloped in his muscular, gentle arms, she refused to let herself think that this man might be involved in something sinister.

Alex was silent on the way back to the office. Sitting next to him on the narrow seat of the electric cart, Gail just managed to maintain a few inches of space between them. He drove slowly this time, as if he were in no hurry at all.

Even so, as they neared the main building, Alex nearly steered the cart head-on into a steel dumpster. Gail grabbed the steering wheel at the last moment to avert an accident. He blinked, as if he had just awakened.

"Alex, you really should lie down before putting on your thinking cap," she told him calmly. "You're a public menace when your mind leaves this planet."

"I was just testing your reflexes," he said distractedly.

"Uh-huh."

They left the cart and entered the building; Gail felt unusually depressed. Apparent sabotage and theft within the Shadow project, in addition to the nagging weaponry question, had thrown a wet blanket onto her initial enthusiasm over the success of the second wind-tunnel test.

The fact that Tom had been excluded from taking part in the second test only added to her dismal mood. When Tom found out, if he didn't already know, that would only add to the ever-widening rift between him and Alex, and, more importantly, between him and Monica. Gail was well aware of the damage her deception was doing to Tom's relationship with her sister. She had to talk to Monica soon, before what they had enjoyed together was damaged beyond repair. She couldn't bear to have that on her conscience.

Alex fidgeted in the elevator, barging out of the cubicle as soon as it opened onto the second floor. He stabbed his identification card into the door lock outside the Shadow project offices, and Gail followed him inside.

They found Tom in his office, his feet up on his desk, obviously seething. Ignoring the withering look in Tom's eyes, Alex marched straight in and slapped the misshapen bolt and the counterfeit sensor unit onto the tan desk blotter.

"Thomas, we have a fox in the henhouse," he said.

Tom glanced down at the items with a noticeable lack of interest. Gail saw his gaze shift briefly to Alex, before settling upon her. She saw the pain behind his anger and felt a stab of guilt.

She should have known better than to enter Tom's office at Alex's side. Tom was already bruised enough to see betrayal in every move she made.

She wondered how she had ever expected to manage Monica's love life, when she hadn't even been able to handle her own. Cliff Danvers had been a shining example of her having two left feet when it came to judging men.

Determined not to let Monica down, Gail moved around the desk to Tom's side. He flinched when she touched him. She gave his forearm a light squeeze, and was relieved when his muscles relaxed. To her surprise and confusion, Alex smiled at her approvingly.

"Well?" Using one finger, Alex nudged the Shadow parts closer to Tom.

Tom took his feet off the desk and sat up in his swivel chair. He folded his arms, so that his right hand covered Gail's, and studied the parts.

"Scrap metal, and an obsolete unit from the microwave sensor," he said impatiently. "What about them?"

"That's a bolt from the anchoring bracket, Tom. It worked itself loose during the failed test," Alex explained.

"Couldn't have," Tom said curtly. "I supervised the anchoring."

"When?"

Tom peered up at Alex, his fingertips digging into the back of Gail's hand. She could see that he was taking Alex's question as a form of accusation.

"I think what Alex is getting at," she said, venturing onto the emotional tightrope strung between the two men, "is that someone must have had access to the drone after your crew secured it."

"Right." Alex nodded. "So when did you finish?"

"Eleven-thirty." Tom rose abruptly. "And nobody got near it afterward, unless he had a high-level security clearance."

He walked to the window and stood with his back to Alex. Alex looked at Gail and motioned her toward Tom. Baffled by the confusing signals she had picked up from him over the past several hours, she went over and slid under Tom's arm.

"As I said, Thomas," Alex repeated, "we have a fox in the henhouse."

Tom pivoted to face him. "Are you pointing a finger at me?"

Gail put an arm around Tom's waist and shook him gently. "Of course not, Tom. You're best friends."

"Oh, yeah?" Tom looked down at her.

Gail felt the heat of his breath on her face. His arm was around her shoulders, but she could sense his icy tension.

"Hold on a darned minute!" Gail suddenly exploded, stepping away from him. "Before we go one step farther, you two idiots better take a good hard look at how much this project is costing you. Because if you ask me, you're paying too high a price, just so a bunch of Pentagon desk jockeys can gloat about having another plaything in their arsenal."

Tom gaped at her for a moment. "Monica?" he asked softly, as if uncertain of what he was hearing.

Gail bit her lip, rocked by her own outburst, certain from Tom's reaction that Monica never lost her temper. But she had meant every word of it and only wished she could get the rest off her chest. She simply did not want to be the disease that killed the long friendship between Tom and Alex, all for the sake of a deception that was growing more hateful to her by the minute.

"Please," she said, her throat constricted with emotion. "Can't we work as a team? This project is beginning to feel like an armed camp."

Tom let her take his hand. His fingers curled around hers, and they both looked at Alex. He stared back at them. After a moment, both men seemed to reach an unspoken truce. Alex extended a hand and picked up the bolt from the desk blotter.

"Tom, after you secured this, someone removed it to get at the wiring," he said, speaking slowly. He watched Tom's brows shoot up before going on.

"Whoever removed and replaced this bolt never expected it to work itself out during the test, in my opinion. Otherwise he wouldn't have bothered to manufacture a wiring short."

"What do you mean, manufacture?" Tom asked, at last beginning to look interested.

"It appears that a very small charge of explosives was set off," Gail told him.

Tom made a surprised sound. "Sabotage?"

"Looks like." Alex tossed aside the bolt and picked up the sensor part. "And if you'll take a closer look at this, you'll see it isn't one of ours. It's counterfeit. I took it out of the model right after the test."

Gail looked at Alex, while Tom frowned at the evidence. Alex hadn't said *after the second test*.

"Someone sabotaged the wiring—" Tom stepped back to his chair "—while someone else was busy stealing a part and replacing it with a counterfeit?" He shook his head. "That's pretty farfetched."

Alex shrugged. "It happened."

After a lengthy silence, Tom asked, "Who?"

Alex spread his hands. "I'll open the floor for nominations."

"Joe Anderson," Gail said, and was surprised at how easily the name popped out.

"Why Joe?" Tom wanted to know.

She turned toward Alex. "While we three were studying the Shadow diagram in your studio at Pinehaven," she explained, "someone went through my luggage. At the time I decided it must have been Joe—or Dorie." She added the last name reluctantly. Gail liked Dorie Pryor.

"Why the hell didn't you say something about this sooner?" Alex demanded.

"Lay off of her, Alex."

Alex spun toward Tom, started to say something, and choked it back.

"If Joe's involved, then it has to be through Dorie," Tom said. "But Dorie doesn't have wind-tunnel security clearance. She doesn't have access to the drone model, once it's installed."

"Maybe she's just passing him the goods," Alex suggested, picking up the counterfeit unit and tossing it back onto the desk. "Maybe she got it from someone else."

"So who switched the part—and planted the explosive charge?" Now Tom picked up the part and tossed it back at him, harder. "Maybe I did it. Is that what you're thinking—*friend?*"

Gail stood watching the uneasy, short-lived truce crumble. "What about Adelaide and me?" she asked, exasperated by their behavior. "And don't forget yourself, Alex. Wouldn't want to leave anybody out of this. And while we're at it, why not toss in the man with the crooked eye? He looks like a real winner. A grease monkey one day, and the next thing you know, he's right there in the middle of the observation party."

Alex stiffened. So did Gail. For the first time, she had blurted out something she couldn't plaster over. She wanted to bolt from the room. Her nerves were too frayed for her to think straight. She imagined she could smell flames licking hungrily at her deception.

Alex took three long strides toward her and grabbed Gail's arm. "What are you talking about, Monica?"

Gail cringed as she saw Alex's reddening face, while Tom stormed around his desk and took her other arm in a viselike hold.

"I said *lay off,* Alex," Tom warned him again.

The two men glared at each other angrily until Gail's arms began aching within their fists. She felt like a chunk of meat between two hungry bulldogs. Alex released her first, opening his hand and then sliding it gently down the inside of her arm.

"All right," Tom said as Alex backed off. "Now let's give Monica time to tell her story."

Gail didn't want to tell anything. But she had opened her big mouth and was left with no choice.

"On the highway near Pinehaven, Friday, I saw a man with one cocked eye changing a tire. At the time I didn't think anything about it." Gail didn't mention that she had stopped to ask the man for directions to Pinehaven. She hadn't lost that much control.

"But I spotted him among the visitors in the wind tunnel this afternoon," she went on.

"I can't believe you waited until now to mention this!" Alex exclaimed. "Who the hell was he?"

"I couldn't see his name tag," Gail said defensively. "As I recall, we were sprinting toward the control center at the time. I guess it just slipped my mind during the test," she added lamely.

Tom finally let go of Gail and went to sit on the corner of his desk. Alex paced the room, rubbing the back of his neck. Tom frowned thoughtfully at Gail, looking slightly puzzled.

Alex stopped at the far side of the room. "Monica, is there anything else that you've been hiding under your hat that we ought to know about?"

Gail laughed mirthlessly to herself. If he only knew. She shook her head. Alex walked toward her, hands in pockets, until he was an arm's length away. He looked carefully at Tom, then bent at the waist and stared hard into her eyes.

"Perhaps you'd like to tell us just why you had to have a week off, right in the heart of the project," he suggested.

Gail blinked rapidly, feeling cornered, and saw Tom rise expectantly. To her astonishment, Alex smiled tauntingly. She looked to Tom for support, but saw that his gaze was riveted on Alex, his puzzlement now tinged with curiosity.

Desperate, Gail knew she had to get out of that room quickly. She also knew that being reasonable wouldn't do the trick, so she retreated into an offensive strategy.

Hands on her hips, she said, "*Dr. Shepard,* I am fed up with this rubbish. I'm also tired and hungry and I have work to do. So, if you'll please excuse me..."

Gail started to leave the room, but Alex grabbed her. His eyes were full of angry amber lights, but his touch was gentle.

"No, *Miss Seabury,*" he said, matching her tone. "I will not excuse you." Alex turned to Tom. "How about that test tomorrow night, Thomas? Did you have any luck persuading Colonel Bryant to help get us scheduled?"

"Tentatively," Tom replied. "But you really ticked him off at the tunnel this afternoon. You're going to have to kiss up to him before it's finalized."

Alex looked colossally pained. "Well, come along, *Miss Seabury.* We have a call to make."

Gail's eyes pleaded with Tom for rescue. But he stood with his arms crossed, scratching his chin as Alex herded her toward the door.

"Wait," Tom said suddenly.

Alex stopped, one hand on the doorknob. Tom tugged pensively at his lower lip, studying them both. Finally he pointed a finger at Gail.

"Dinner as usual tonight?" he asked.

Startled, Gail almost muffed her response. Obviously Tom and Monica had some kind of standing dinner date. She nodded dumbly, wondering how she would ever make it through an entire evening alone with Tom, without being found out. The deception already had left her exhausted.

Alex opened the door and escorted her out. As they walked the short distance down the corridor to his office, he stroked the inside of her arm with his thumb. Her pulse quickened, even as alarms went off inside her head.

"Tom's the most decent human being I've ever known," Alex said unexpectedly.

Gail wondered if the two men had that quality in common. Then she remembered her unanswered question. Was the Shadow a potential weapon? Suddenly she felt queasy.

When she said nothing, Alex added, "We get toe-to-toe with each other a lot, because we're both bullheaded. But Tom's the closest thing I have to a brother."

He kept stroking her arm, sending pleasure chills throughout her body. When he paused to open his office door, Gail looked angrily at Alex, asking herself what kind of man would have the gall to make moves on his best friend's lover. He met her gaze with a bafflingly playful smile.

"WHAT WENT WRONG this afternoon?" Dorie asked, without looking up from her computer terminal.

"I'd like to know that myself," Adelaide replied tersely. "Colonel Bryant was fit to be tied after the test failure. But instead of smoothing his ruffled feathers, Monica sniped right back at him."

"Really?" Dorie tilted her head to one side. "That doesn't sound like Monica." She twisted down one corner of her mouth. "Have you noticed that she's quit smoking?"

"That explains her behavior since she's been back." Adelaide came to stand behind Dorie, peering past her shoulder at the orange readout on the video display. "How are you coming with the new figures Alex gave you?"

"Finished. But honestly, Adelaide, I don't see why he keeps fine-tuning his design changes when they haven't figured out what caused the failure yet. And we don't even know if the test can be rescheduled by tomorrow night."

"You let Alex and Tom worry about that," Adelaide said sharply. "You just do your job."

Dorie hunched her shoulders, stung by the criticism. She quickly removed the floppy disk from her terminal's drive and handed it to Adelaide. Sometimes the woman could be such a jerk.

"Did you do a backup copy of this?" Adelaide asked.

"Of course," Dorie said wearily. When Adelaide was on a roll, she seemed to take perverse pleasure in treating everyone like a moron.

"Where is it?" Adelaide strummed her fingers impatiently on the floppy-disk packet.

"Alex popped in and took it while you were meeting with Tom awhile ago. He said he'd bring it back and lock it in the vault before he left this evening."

Adelaide looked annoyed, which gave Dorie a surge of satisfaction. She watched Adelaide wheel around and march over to the locked door to the Confidential Data room.

"Shadow," Adelaide said, pausing at the door.

The voice-activated lock, which was programmed for entry by only a handful of the project's team members, disengaged. The door popped open slightly, and Adelaide moved inside. For once she didn't close the door behind her.

Dorie was tempted to take a peek inside at the data vault. She had always resented not being among the chosen few who could come and go through that door at will. But if Adelaide caught her looking, she might become suspicious, and Adelaide was already difficult enough to get along with.

Not that a simple peek would be worth anything. There were a jillion little half-hidden security barriers in the Shadow project, designed to preserve the ignorance of the ignorant. For example, Dorie was never permitted to see a full set of data on any Shadow computer model. She was allowed to work up the model only so far, then Adelaide personally inserted the final, crucial elements.

So it stood to reason that if she did sneak over and take a peek through that open door into the data room, Dorie wouldn't see much. Probably just a wall of unlabeled file vaults, possibly with the latest fingerprint-decoding locks. At least, she liked to think it was something that sophisticated, and not just a cardboard box sitting on a table. Anyway, finding out wasn't worth the risk of becoming a burr under Adelaide's saddle.

Besides, Dorie knew she couldn't pass up this opportunity. It was almost quitting time, and she might not get another chance.

She kicked her canvas purse from under the desk and quickly opened the lower drawer. With one eye on the Confidential Data room, she hastily slipped a floppy disk from the drawer and into her purse.

Adelaide reappeared just as she closed the drawer. She noticed Dorie's purse on the floor and scowled.

"Leaving already?" Adelaide asked.

"Unless you need me to hang around for anything else," Dorie said, her heart pounding. "Joe's picking me up."

Her mention of Joe seemed to strike a sour note. Adelaide glanced around the room, as if trying to come up with another job that would keep Dorie's nose to the grindstone awhile longer.

Dorie cast a furtive look at her purse, feeling her palms dampen. She was absurdly convinced that Adelaide would use her X-ray vision and spot the stolen disk.

Adelaide sighed. "Go ahead."

Dorie shouldered the strap on her purse and walked swiftly to the door. She hurried down the corridor to the elevator, feeling as though she was being chased, expecting the alarm to be raised at any moment. The feeling clung to her all the way to the front security gate.

Seeing Joe's pickup parked at the curb on the other side of the kiosk did little to assuage her sense of impending disaster. Only when she was past the vehicle barrier, was she able to breathe easily.

Joe reached across the truck cab and opened the door for her, his face very close to hers as she climbed into the seat. "Rough day?" he inquired.

"Yeah. I'm bushed." Dorie tried to lighten her expression. But from the sympathetic look Joe gave her, she knew it wasn't working.

She dumped her purse onto the seat between them and rested her head back, closing her eyes and groaning. He moved close, then his warm lips were on hers. She returned his kiss, wondering how much longer this could go on.

A moment later, Joe pulled away from the gate, swung through the curve of the driveway, and headed toward her apartment complex. Dorie stared through the windshield most of the way. They had almost reached her place when she nudged her purse as if by accident. The flap fell open, revealing the floppy disk.

Dorie watched Joe out of the corner of her eye. He drove on for another block, his jaw muscles bunched. Then he reached over and picked up the disk without looking at it. As he slipped it into his inside coat pocket, Dorie turned her face to the side window, biting her lip so hard that she tasted blood in her mouth.

CHAPTER ELEVEN

ALEX WAS PAINFULLY AWARE that Gail had barely spoken to him since leaving his office, following the call to Colonel Bryant. He stood at his drawing board, drinking brackish reheated coffee from a foam cup, trying to force his priorities into some sense of order.

Gail kept commandeering the number one spot. And the longer this crazy mess lasted, the more he was coming to think of her as Gail and not Monica. In a weird sort of way, Alex thought, it was like becoming bilingual.

Regardless of what he called her in his mind, the lady was fuming, and he couldn't blame her. For some reason that Alex couldn't quite understand, he had intentionally baited her in front of Tom. She had handled it well, but the strain certainly hadn't won Alex any points with her.

Maybe it was better this way, until the crucial Shadow tests were over. He couldn't cope with tomorrow night while still trying to deal with the sudden reality of his feelings for her.

Alex slam-dunked the cup into a nearby wastebasket. Life could be damned unfair. He was on the verge of being happy, really knocked-out happy, and it could very well be at his best friend's expense. Where *was* Monica? He combed a hand through his tousled hair, wondering if she was even still alive. Dick Brady didn't seem to have a clue.

His hand wandered to the tender wound at his temple. If the worst had happened to Monica, how would Tom handle knowing that Alex had fallen in love with their pseudo-Monica? Would just looking at Gail be a cruel reminder to Tom of a love that was forever lost to him?

And what about Gail herself? She might already have lost the sister she had never known. Alex paced the room. If Monica was at risk—in danger—then surely Gail was in equal peril. The mere thought made his blood run cold.

"Alex?"

"What?" he snapped, whirling.

Adelaide's head stuck through a narrow opening in the doorway, looking disembodied. Alex slowly wiped a hand across his forehead.

"Sorry, Adelaide. You startled me."

"You didn't exactly go down like a glass of warm milk yourself," she said, shaking her head. "Before she left, Dorie told me you had the backup disk with the design refinements."

"Dorie's already gone?" Alex frowned.

Adelaide nodded resignedly. "Joe picked her up."

Joe and Dorie. Dorie and Joe. Alex ran the names back and forth through his mind, not liking the way they sounded together. Maybe that was just his imagination, but he couldn't afford to be charitable.

He pointed to the floppy disk on his desk. Adelaide glanced at it and shook her head.

"I'm not on a search-and-seizure mission, Alex. I just want to make sure you remember to put it in the data vault before you leave."

"Take it." Alex ripped a sheet of paper from the drawing board. "Take this, too. If you can incorporate this new material into the disk data before you abandon ship for the night, I'll be hugely indebted to you."

"You already are," Adelaide said sternly.

She winked broadly at him, and Alex chuckled in spite of himself. He never ceased to be amazed by these little reminders that Adelaide did have a sense of humor, however deeply she kept it buried.

"You're something, Adelaide," he told her. "How would we manage without you?"

"Badly, Alex. Very badly."

With that she was gone. Alex wandered into the corridor. Still pondering the Dorie-Joe situation, he didn't realize he had stopped in front of Monica's door until it opened.

"Oh!" Gail gasped as she ran into him.

"Don't you watch where you're going?" he asked, rubbing his ribs where she had jabbed him with the notebook she was carrying.

"Don't you watch where you're standing?" she fired back.

She stared at his chest, waiting for him to move. Alex wanted to reach out and pull her into his arms, shielding her from—what? Shadow's vicious gremlins?

Gail glanced past him, a look of relief replacing her strained expression. Alex stepped to one side as Tom joined them.

"Six-thirty?" Tom asked Gail.

She nodded, smiling, and Alex felt a stab of jealousy. How much did Gail Montgomery like Tom, and how much was just role-playing? He couldn't tell, but the fact that he was afraid about it made him angry at himself.

"Tom, I just gave Adelaide some final input for the drone," he said formally. "We'll be installing a new component package in that forward compartment before tomorrow night's test."

Tom flared. "What kind of component?"

"We'll discuss that later," Alex said evasively. "The important thing right now is that you have the drone model ready to accept it by noon tomorrow, now that the test schedule has been confirmed."

He saw Tom turn away slightly and glare at the wall, visibly struggling to corral his temper. Alex waited tensely for the explosion, wishing that he could come right out and tell Tom everything. But he had already given his word to Brady. Finding out the truth about Gail had cost Alex his freedom to choose whom to trust and when.

"All right, Alex," Tom said icily. "I'll have the model ready on schedule. But after tomorrow night's test, I think you'd better find yourself another project test manager."

He started to walk away. Alex stopped him, and Tom spun back around, fists clenched. Alex released him, alarmed that Tom might actually take a swing at him.

"Easy, *amigo*," Alex said earnestly. "I know this looks as if I'm trying to shut you out. But bear with me just another day or so. This will work out, I swear."

Tom looked from Alex to Gail. "This is rich," he said, smiling sadly through his anger. "You two are starting to sound just alike."

Alex wasn't sure what he was talking about, but had a pretty good idea. He figured Gail must have been keeping Tom at arm's length, these past several days, and Tom was none too happy about it. For the first time Alex fully appreciated the complexity of her predicament.

"Thomas, please," he said, still agonizing over being handcuffed by his promise to Brady. "There are two sides to everything."

He looked down at Gail, who was eyeing him closely, then shifted his gaze to Tom so he wouldn't have to look at her. He was close to telling Brady to shove it, so he could spill everything to Tom and Gail and end this burlesque once and for all.

While Alex was wrestling with that thought, Tom turned again and walked away, his fists still clenched. Gail turned to Alex, her smoky eyes smoldering.

"Alex, if you can't believe in your best friend, who can you believe in?" she asked, tight-lipped.

Before Alex could reply, Gail hurried off after Tom. Alex watched her catch up with him at the end of the corridor. Tom stopped, and they spoke in hushed tones for a moment. When Tom finally shook his head wearily and put an arm around Gail's shoulders, Alex felt a dull ache rise into his chest.

AN HOUR LATER, Alex entered Adelaide's office. She glanced up from her computer terminal as he sagged into Dorie's desk chair. Punching a button to dump whatever she had been working on, she swiveled to face him.

"Let me guess," she said, auditing his expression. "Heartburn and a headache."

"Close. Very close."

"You can't live on coffee, Alex. And when was the last time you had any sleep?"

"What day is this?"

"I thought so." Adelaide heaved herself out of her chair and reached into a small portable refrigerator perched atop a filing cabinet. "Here, try nutrition for a change."

To humor her, Alex accepted a small plastic container of orange juice. He shook it up, peeled off the lid and took a swig.

"Ugh!" He made a face. "Tastes like liquid plastic with a dash of battery acid."

Adelaide swatted him with a sheaf of papers. "If you don't start taking better care of yourself, we'll be feeding you through a tube in your arm."

As he tipped up the bottle to finish it off, Alex noticed the door to the Confidential Data room standing slightly ajar. "What's that doing open?" he asked.

"Good Lord!" Adelaide exclaimed, visibly chagrined. "I must be getting sloppy in my old age." She leaned a formidable hip into the door, and the lock engaged with an audible click.

"You haven't been leaving it unlocked, have you?"

"Nope," she said, settling back into her seat.

But Alex thought he detected a deepening of the frown line between her eyes. He sighed. "I sincerely hope not, Adelaide. I'm beginning to think you're the only stable element left in the Shadow project.''

Adelaide laughed huskily. ''Your design changes certainly have Tom bucking in the traces. But you still have Monica to count on.''

Alex stared broodingly into the empty bottle and made no comment. He heard Adelaide clear her throat.

''Alex, this is none of my business, but is there something going on between you and Monica?''

His head snapped up. ''What makes you think that?''

''Because ever since we returned from Pinehaven, you and Tom have been like two big stags preparing to duke it out over a single doe.''

''That's the most ridiculous thing I've ever heard!'' he exclaimed, flabbergasted. Was his attraction to Gail that obvious? Alex was starting to add another layer to his denial, when the office door opened and Gail entered.

Alex and Adelaide turned to look at her. Gail could tell from their expressions that they had been talking about her. She closed the door behind her, pretending she hadn't noticed.

''Alex, I'm knocking off for the day,'' she said. ''I can come back later in the evening, if you need me.''

The aloofness in her tone told Alex that Gail was still miffed at the way he had shut out Tom. If Adelaide hadn't been sitting there, he would have been sorely tempted to tell Gail he wasn't exactly thrilled about being shut out of her part in this little farce, either. Reminding himself that Gail's options were as limited as his own, he restrained himself.

"Go ahead and enjoy dinner," he said instead. "You and Tom deserve it."

Alex saw Gail glance at Adelaide and sensed that Gail hadn't come just to tell him she was on her way home. Something else was bothering her. He rose and offered her Dorie's chair. Gail shook her head, but Alex remained standing, sensing the gravity of her mood.

"I have a problem with Shadow, Alex," she said finally, rubbing her palms together.

Alex nodded for her to go on.

"I've put a lot of thought into that new component." Gail glanced at Adelaide again, struggling with her tension. "I think you both know what I'm talking about."

He recalled her asking him whether the new component was some kind of offensive weapon. The question had floored him and Alex now regretted not having given her some kind of answer at the time.

"Adelaide doesn't know about it," he told her. "The computer model you worked up for me today hasn't been interfaced with Adelaide's."

Gail's eyes widened and she winced, as if she knew she had let a cat out of the bag. Adelaide simply recrossed her legs and leaned an elbow on her desk.

"Come now, Alex," she said, clearly interested. "What have you been holding out on me?"

Alex gave himself all the time in the world to think about it, aware that both women were staring at him. Shadow was roughly thirty hours from its final wind-tunnel test. Regardless of the rules that Brady had laid down as to what Alex could tell the team members, each and every one of them had a right to know just how much was riding on the outcome of the test.

Alex needed more than just their hard work. He needed the extra measure of trust and loyalty that added up to 110 percent. Having almost lost that from Tom, his vital right arm, he couldn't afford to risk more.

"Dammit, if I can't trust you two," he said, "we might as well fold our tent and go home."

As a member of Brady's own team, he reasoned, Gail was beyond reproach. And Adelaide had been privy to Shadow's deepest secrets—except for one—since the very beginning.

"Sit down, Monica," Adelaide said. "I do believe our intrepid leader is about to lay his cards on the table."

Alex watched Gail cross to Dorie's chair. She had that nervous look about her again, an aura of alertness—tension—that made him want to hover over her like a hawk protecting its young. Yet he sensed an inner strength in her, too, that he deeply admired.

"You can forget about getting the whole dog and pony show, Adelaide," he said. "All I can give you is the nutshell."

"Fire away." Adelaide leaned forward expectantly.

He looked at Gail, sitting on the edge of her chair, still wide-eyed. Whatever lingering doubts he might have had about being totally honest with these two women fell by the wayside. "You've had a hand in developing all of Shadow's operational software, Adelaide," he began. "You're also familiar with the drone's classified design."

Adelaide nodded impatiently.

"What you haven't yet seen is a component that Tom's crew will install tomorrow. It *is* a weapon." He watched Gail's face go pale. "Of sorts."

Adelaide appeared to be hypnotized, her eyes riveted on him. Gail lowered her head and stared down at her tightly clasped hands.

"The component is a simple, relatively cheap system—a sort of grass-roots Star Wars—capable of electronically jamming missiles in their launchers."

Gail's head came up slowly, her full lips slightly parted. Alex winked at her, not caring if Adelaide noticed. Seeing the color rise in Gail's cheeks like the blush on a peach was like a tonic.

"One question each," he said. "No guaranteed answers."

Adelaide jumped in first. "Is this some kind of antiterrorist device?"

Alex shrugged. "More like antimissile, period. It can have all sorts of applications. For instance, it could enable commercial airliners to fly unscathed over almost any territory."

He turned to Gail, wondering what her engineer's mind would do with the concept. But her question came straight out of left field.

"Why did you tell us about this, Alex?"

"Because the personal danger level involved with this project is getting out of hand," he said. "Especially since the break-in at your place last night. You all need to know how important this thing is, not just to us, but to the real world out there."

"It's an incredible breakthrough, Alex," Adelaide said. "Surely the air force wouldn't cancel our contract, when we're this close to perfecting the Shadow?"

Alex shook his head. "Tom claims that Weissman Aircraft is on the verge of producing a similar drone. The first one to cross the finish line gets the go-ahead."

"Then it wasn't an accident?" Gail wanted to know.

"What?" Alex saw her staring at the wound on his forehead. "The tree? Who knows?" Alex was sure now that it had been no accident, but wasn't ready to openly acknowledge that. Not with the look of sick dread in Gail's eyes. "What would anyone want from me?"

"Your life," Gail said after a short pause.

Before Alex could react, she jumped up and brushed past him. She flung open the door and disappeared down the corridor.

"What was that all about?" he asked no one in particular.

He saw Adelaide take a deep breath and turn back to her terminal. "I'm not sure, Alex," she said, striking a key to pull up a menu. "But I sure will be glad when this circus is over."

THIS HAD BEEN the longest day of her life, Gail thought, pulling out of the parking area. She had an overwhelming need to talk to Monica. In an odd sort of way, finding out the truth about Shadow's mystery component had only made that need stronger.

When Alex had explained the component to them, Gail could have leaped up and thrown her arms around him. Her sense of relief had been almost like a rebirth. Then her dilemma had reared its ugly head, right in her face.

To him she was Monica. And after tomorrow night's test, when Alex found out her true identity, she would be absolutely nothing to him. Worse than nothing. He would look upon her as something vile and deceitful.

Gail drove through the security gate and accelerated onto the road leading toward town. In spite of her preoccupation, she couldn't help being aware of the parklike scenery surrounding the facility. A young white-tailed deer grazed by the roadway. As she drew near, his head came up with a jerk. He watched for a moment with alert round eyes, ears twitching. Then he lowered his head again, appearing to see no cause for alarm in the swift red Porsche. The scene reminded Gail of Pinehaven, and she felt her chin quiver.

She entered Monica's apartment minutes later and glanced at her watch. She was cutting it close. Tom would be picking her up in less than twenty minutes.

The thought of spending the evening with Monica's lover filled her with a special kind of dread. If Gail played her cards Tom's way, for Monica's sake, she might be able to save the relationship that seemed to be crumbling hourly in her twin's absence. But Gail knew she couldn't possibly surrender herself to Tom's ardor. Nonetheless, she had no idea what she *would* do.

Gail showered quickly and grabbed clothes from Monica's closet. She was just applying a touch of gray eye shadow, when Tom knocked on the door. Taking a deep breath to quell the flutter in her stomach, she hurried to greet him.

"Why didn't you let yourself in?" she asked, forcing a cheerful smile.

Tom shrugged, but she could see the answer in his face. He had lost confidence in his relationship with Monica.

"You look great," he told her admiringly.

He sounded nervous, like a new suitor. Ashamed of her deception and filled with sympathy for what Tom was going through, Gail hugged him with genuine affection. It was a measure of the man, she reflected, that even though she hadn't yet gotten used to having a sister, she was already looking forward to having Tom as a brother-in-law.

"That's because you always make me feel great," she replied.

Tom smiled hopefully and pulled her closer. But as his hands roamed up and down her back, Gail couldn't help tensing at his prelude to intimacy. He abruptly pulled away from her, his smile replaced with a look of pained frustration. Gail had a feeling it was going to be a long evening.

"I'm so tired, Tom," she said, hoping he would take that as the reason for her resistance to his advances.

His lips tightened. "Are you calling off dinner?"

"No!" She tugged at the front of his shirt, trying to keep their physical contact harmlessly playful. "You aren't getting out of it, buster. I'm starving."

"Good." Tom closed her apartment door, and they started toward the elevator. "It's your turn to pick the place."

Gail blanched. The evening had barely begun, and Monica and Tom's little traditions were already killing her. She hadn't the faintest idea what foods they liked. And the only eatery that she remembered seeing in town was a McDonald's out on the highway. She was half tempted to say she was having a Big Mac attack.

"Ribs," she said instead, glancing at Tom to gauge his reaction.

He looked at her askance as he ushered her into the elevator. "You're serious? Adam's Rib? I thought you hated the place."

From his surprised-but-pleased expression, Gail deduced that she had hit the jackpot. With the odds stacked heavily against her, she had lucked onto just the right choice.

"Tastes change." She grinned. "I woke up this morning craving ribs."

"Ain't life strange?" he said, visibly bemused.

Gail began to relax on the drive across town and discovered that Tom could be good company. He was more attentive than Alex, perhaps because he was trying so hard to figure out why she wasn't responding to him as Monica would.

She caught herself comparing Tom with Alex. It was like stacking up a rainbow against a glaring white light. One touched her heart, and the other somehow reached deep down into her soul. At the moment, both men were causing her a world of heartache.

The head waiter at the rib joint called Tom by name and showed them to a table with a window view of an apricot sunset. The lighting was dim, with a candle flickering inside a ruby glass dome on the table. Tom held her hand as they studied the menu. Gail had trouble reading, with his index finger drawing little curlicues on her palm and wished she'd chosen a less romantic setting.

"I owe you an apology," Tom said later, while they waited for their dinner to be served.

"For what?" Gail had finally managed to remove her hand from his, on the pretext of dusting non-existent lint from the lapel of his sport coat.

"For last night," he said ruefully. "When Adelaide told me about the break-in at your apartment, I could have slit my throat." He shook his head. "What a time to get bombed out of my gourd."

Gail touched his sleeve. He didn't look at her. She realized for the first time that this was something that had been eating at him all day.

"Can you forgive me for not being there when you needed me?" he asked.

"There's nothing to forgive," she said softly. "It was no big deal. Honest."

"I know better than that. Alex told me you were petrified when he got there."

"You two talked about it?" Gail asked, surprised.

"Yeah. Late this afternoon. You know how subtle Alex is. He came right out and told me I was behaving like a first-class dork."

"How rude!"

"Rude, but true. I would have decked him for it, but then he took off on a tangent. Started talking in circles." Tom frowned, trying to recall details of their conversation.

"First he said something about being in the same boat with me, sailing on two separate oceans. Then he got into different kinds of peaches looking a lot alike, but not tasting the same. He said I shouldn't get him wrong—he might prefer one over the other, but that didn't make his choice necessarily superior to mine. People just had different tastes, that's all."

"I'm having trouble following that," Gail admitted.

"So did I. Believe me, Monica, he sounded downright bizarre." Tom frowned. "And he kept looking at me real intensely, as if he were expecting me to read his mind or something."

"What do you suppose Alex was getting at?"

"I couldn't begin to guess," he told her. "Except that I got the distinct impression that it had something to do with you."

Tom looked at her searchingly. Gail returned his gaze, totally mystified.

"I asked him if his concussion was rebounding on him," Tom went on. "He acted real frustrated then. He said he couldn't spell it out any clearer—which made no sense at all to me. Then he told me to just relax and hang tough, because he had it on good authority that there was going to be a helluva peach crop this year."

"You didn't leave him alone, did you?" Gail asked, suddenly worried. "Maybe it's the concussion."

Tom shook his head. "I don't know. He looked so blasted . . . happy. To be honest, that kind of got my goat." He sighed and sat toying with his glass.

"Do you think he should be examined by a doctor?" Gail blinked away the sickening vision of Alex sprawled in the clearing next to the fallen tree.

"You'd have to find him first," Tom said. "He took off to some kind of meeting. Wouldn't tell me where it was or what it was about."

His last comment jolted Gail. She wondered if Alex had told Tom about the purpose of the new component. She was trying to decide if she should ask, when the waiter placed an enormous platter of barbecued ribs in front of her.

They ate in silence for awhile. Gail's thoughts repeatedly drifted to Alex, and each time she had to drag them back again. She ate more than she wanted, just to keep from having to talk.

"You never did say if you've forgiven me," Tom said over their after-dinner coffee.

"There's nothing to forgive, Tom. We've all been under a great deal of strain lately. Each of us reacts in a different way. You went out and got a snootful. Alex has started talking like a crazy man."

"And you quit smoking." Tom glanced pointedly at the clean, ruby glass ashtray with a book of matches propped in the middle.

Gail almost dropped her coffee cup. Nobody had mentioned to her that Monica smoked.

"You noticed," she said, bluffing a wry smile.

"I notice everything about you, Monica." Tom reached for her hand. "The fact is, lately I've been noticing a lot of things about you."

Tom gazed into her eyes, and Gail prayed that he wouldn't see the pandemonium that he had just unleashed within her. Her heart skipped a beat, then took off as if she were doing wind sprints.

"What kind of things?" she finally dared to ask.

"Nothing special. Little things." Tom's gaze remained plugged into Gail's. "The smoking. You haven't called me Tommy since you got back. You ate dessert." He suddenly looked uncomfortable. "You don't seem the least bit interested in touching my body."

Gail thrashed around in her mind for something to say. She could come up with plenty of individual explanations. But she couldn't seem to find a plausible one for the collection of differences Tom had compiled.

"Maybe I'm just having an identity crisis," she said lamely.

Tom looked at her for a long time. Gail watched the light in his eyes fade, horrified by the prospect that his feelings for Monica might be dying before her very eyes.

"Please, Tom," she said, pleading for Monica with all her heart. "Give me time. I love you so much."

He kept staring at her, not speaking. Finally he said, "It's getting late. We'd better pack it in."

Gail sat close to Tom on the drive back to Monica's apartment, smiling up at him whenever he looked at her. She patted his hand when he placed it on her knee—silently praying that it wouldn't start roaming—and tried to make light and witty conversation.

The more she prattled, the more she joked and played the role of his significant other, the harder he just looked at her. She found his silence unnerving.

By the time they reached the apartment complex, Gail felt as if she were playing a one-woman Ping-Pong match. She wasn't expecting Tom to break the silence with a challenge.

"Are you going to tell me why I was left out of this afternoon's second wind-tunnel test?" he asked.

Gail closed her eyes, her thought processes slamming head-on into a new obstacle. She desperately wanted to crawl into a hole somewhere and never come out.

"I don't know why," she said, falling back on pure honesty. "Alex seemed to get the bit in his teeth, and there was no stopping him."

Tom double-parked behind Monica's Porsche. Gail kept expecting him to resurrect the subject as they crossed the parking lot and rode the elevator up to her floor. She was relieved when he didn't.

He used his key to unlock her door. Gail turned to face him on the threshold, knowing that she was confronting a moment of truth. Tom stood for a moment, tracing the line of her jaw with the back of one finger.

"Are you going to invite me in?" he asked.

Gail hesitated. "I've had a lovely evening, Tom. But I'm just too bushed to make a night of it."

Tom's hand drifted to the side of her face, brushing back the hair from her ear. He bent to kiss her exposed earlobe—and suddenly straightened.

"Uh...you're right, sugar," he said. "It's late, and we all have a big day tomorrow."

"Tom, are you angry?" Gail placed a hand on his chest, nonplussed by his sudden about-face.

"No. Me? No."

On second thought, Gail decided that he didn't look angry. He looked rattled. But then he seemed to pull himself together.

"Look, Monica," he said, moving away from her, "this is no good. We can't keep on like this."

"Tom, I need time," she said, feeling like a broken record. Gail reached for him, but he backed up another step, still with an unsettled look in his dark eyes.

"Take all the time you need," he said. "I'll not hold you to any of the promises we've made to each other."

Gail sucked in her breath. "Tom, are you calling off our engagement?"

"For the time being." He nodded. "Maybe we can take another look at it later."

Gail started to protest, heartsick at the thought of Monica set adrift with Tom's unborn child. But he placed a silencing finger across her lips.

"Sleep tight, princess," he said softly, and a distant cloud seemed to pass behind his eyes.

While she tried to frame a suitable endearment that wouldn't give this parting such a sense of finality, Tom turned and strode off down the hallway. He looked back at her twice before reaching the elevator.

Gail remained in the doorway long after he was gone. She had expected an unpleasant scene when she turned Tom away from her door and bed. Instead, he had seemed perfectly satisfied with the rebuff. Even his release of Monica had been strangely without anger.

Was he finally giving up on the relationship?

CHAPTER TWELVE

ALEX STOOD in the dimly lighted hallway outside Monica's apartment. In his right hand he held two perfect roses, one white one and one red. He knocked softly, waited, then knocked again.

Gail opened the door. Anxiety was written all over her face. Her mouth fell open.

"Going to bed so early?" Alex asked, holding out the roses to her. A hint of laughter brightened his warm gaze as it swept the length of Monica's satin-trimmed robe.

"It's been a trying day," Gail said, still dazed by his appearance at her door.

She hesitated, then reached for the roses. Alex didn't release them at once. For several electric seconds they held the stems together, their hands touching.

When his hand finally dropped away, Gail cupped the velvetlike petals in her hand and inhaled their heady fragrance. "What are these for?" she asked.

"What are roses always for?" Alex smiled playfully.

Gail looked at him quizzically. He seemed to be teasing her. Yet something in his eyes sent a deep quiver through her.

She stepped back, and he moved inside. When she closed the door, Alex's presence filled the room. Gail couldn't think clearly. The roses and Alex's relentless gaze were just too much.

"Why two?" she managed at last, fingering the delicate petals.

"They're symbolic," he said. "The white one is for purity." The purity of the dream, he thought, as the woman standing before him seemed to merge with the portrait that he kept in his bedroom at Pinehaven. "And doesn't red always signify passion?"

His voice drifted down to a near whisper, his gaze again gliding over the curves and folds of Monica's robe. Gail's breath hitched in her chest. His impish smile softened, but still the lights danced in the amber depths of his eyes.

"I'd better go find a vase," she said, convinced that her voice sounded strangely constricted. She fled the room.

Safely in the kitchen, she grabbed hold of the countertop, swaying dizzily, and stared down at the roses. What had Alex meant by purity? And what about passion? In fact, what did he mean by being here at all?

Gail turned on the faucet, wet the corner of a dish towel, and held it to her throat. As her nerves began to calm, she hurriedly rummaged through the cabinets.

When she returned to the living room, Alex was standing at the French doors, staring out at the darkness. She placed the cut glass vase containing the roses on a small end table.

"I don't know what to say, Alex," she told him. Would it be proper, she wondered, to thank him for bringing roses to the woman whom he knew as his best friend's fiancée?

Alex turned. "You don't need to say anything."

The instant their gazes met, she felt something dangerously sensual flowing between them and found it impossible to look away. Instead she stood motionless, letting him drink her in, feeling a warm glow spread over her body.

He took a step toward her, and Gail suddenly pulled back. This was crazy! What was happening to her? She moved quickly to one side so that a wing chair stood between them, her heart trip-hammering wildly.

"Tom just left." She gripped the back of the chair, feeling compelled for Monica's sake to hold Tom in front of her like a shield.

Alex smiled again, as if he knew exactly what she was doing, and nodded. ''I passed him on the highway.''

The French doors rattled behind him. Gail jumped, distracted. Raindrops tapped erratically against the glass, and were followed by a distant rumble of thunder.

''It's blowing up a good storm outside,'' he said, casually moving away from the door.

Gail nodded, aware of a different kind of storm brewing inside. Alex stopped to touch the roses on the table.

''Shall I leave?'' he asked in a hushed tone.

Gail swallowed dryly. ''Why did you come, Alex?''

He kept moving around the room, one ambling step at a time, touching things. The ornate ashtray next to the bud vase. A marble paperweight on the cherry-wood desk. Monica's suede jacket, which Gail had left draped over the back of the couch. Before she realized that she had been disarmed by his seemingly aimless wandering, Alex was standing next to her.

''I'm not very smooth at explaining myself,'' he confessed, a slight tremor in his voice betraying his own tension. ''Maybe I should just show you why I came.''

His big hand covered hers on the back of the chair. He bent and touched his lips briefly to hers, and Gail felt the dizziness return. His voice seemed to come from a great distance.

"I never knew I could love someone so much," he whispered, his lips inches from hers. "Every time I close my eyes, I dream of you. And when I open them, there you are, as warm and real as the sun." Again his lips brushed hers. "I had to come. It's so cold out there."

Gail's knees turned to jelly. His arms went around her, and she stood with her hands on his shoulders, struggling to maintain the last vestiges of her self-control.

A clap of thunder drove her deeper into his embrace, her arms flying around his neck. Alex held her tightly, his cheek pressed against hers; Gail's toes barely touched the carpet.

"Oh, Alex," she murmured, her mind reeling. Who was she? Gail? Monica? Had she completely lost her sanity and become both her sister and herself? "Alex, I love you with all my heart."

He pushed her gently away from him, so he could look into her eyes. "For real?" he asked hoarsely.

Gail stroked her fingers through the hair behind his ears and stepped off the tightrope she had been walking for days. She was Gail. With his arms encircling her and passion shining in his eyes, she had no will to be anyone but herself.

"For real," she whispered.

Alex kissed her again, softly at first, then with deepening hunger, his breath shuddering as they clung to each other. Gail had never wanted a man the way she wanted Alex now. Their lips parted, and she took his hand into her own.

"Will you stay?" she asked, her voice barely audible above the rising storm.

For a moment he seemed too stunned by their kiss to comprehend. Then his thumb traced a line from her earlobe down the side of her neck, sending an exquisite bolt of lightning through her.

"Are you sure?" he inquired softly.

"I've never been more sure of anything in my life."

She led him across the threshold into the bedroom, and when she turned toward him again, Alex seemed to sense the nervousness underlying her desire. He took her into his arms with great gentleness, as if cradling a fragile treasure.

The next hour slipped by like a shadow. Gail lay beside Alex, loving the feel of his smooth, taut skin quivering under her sensitive fingers, needing to give as well as receive love. Surrendering to the devastating ecstasy of his kisses, she felt wantonly alive, soaring high like the Shadow itself into the singing stratosphere, turning, twisting, diving, dipping in arcs of unending pleasure. The tender yet feverish movements of his hands, lips and tongue explored the uncivilized canyons of her mind. Their bodies came together with whispered words of love that swept them deeper, higher and farther than either had ever been before.

Later they lay satiated in each other's arms, listening to rain patter from the eaves outside the window. Alex gently stroked her hair. Gail's hand rested on his thick chest, feeling his powerful heartbeat against her palm.

"I love you, my darling," he said.

"And I love you." Gail touched the sculpted outline of his lips with a fingertip.

She felt him smile. In one smooth motion he rolled over and pressed his lips to hers, one hand resting on the curve of her hip. Gail returned his kiss with an entire new arsenal of emotions, feeling completely whole in his sensuous embrace.

The shrilling of the telephone on the bedside table broke harshly into their reawakening passion. Alex bolted upright. The phone rang again, and Gail slithered under his arm to reach for it.

"Hello?"

"Gail, it's me."

Monica! Gail almost dropped the receiver. She turned her back to Alex and moved to the edge of the bed. His hand followed her hip.

"Uh...hello?" she said again, feeling bug-eyed at being blessed with a call from her sister at the worst possible time.

As if sensing Gail's desperate dilemma, Monica lowered her voice. "Sis, are you alone?"

"No, I'm not," Gail said in the slight singsong of a polite person talking to a complete stranger.

"I thought sure you would be at this hour," Monica said. With a trace of apology she added, "You aren't in bed with someone, are you?"

"Yes, I am," Gail said politely, smiling into the darkness.

After what seemed like an eternity, a single word wafted fearfully into Gail's ear. "Tom?"

"No!" Alex's hand moved from Gail's hip to the hollow of her waist.

"Whew! You had me going there for a second." Monica's relief was audible. "Then who the devil . . . ?"

"It could be a friend," Gail said ambiguously, hearing her voice catching as Alex's thumb traveled from the base of her spine to the nape of her neck.

"Not Alex!"

"Well, yes."

To Gail's consternation Monica laughed. "I can't believe you broke through the man's monolithic barriers so fast." Monica was silent for a moment, then added soberly, "On second thought, maybe I was the barrier basher and didn't know it."

Gail's entire body went rigid. Alex eased closer against her and began massaging her shoulders. She wanted to scream at him to stop; the impact of Monica's words had shattered the almost spiritual sensuality that Gail had shared with Alex only moments earlier.

"I'm afraid you'll have to redial," she said, suddenly feeling as if she were suffocating.

Gail had longed for this call, stockpiling a thousand questions with which to bombard her sister. Now she lay trapped between the man she loved—and the woman he loved. With horror she glimpsed the long, black tunnel of grief that stretched into her future.

"I understand, Sis," Monica went on. "I just wanted you to know I've found a way to contact my supervisor without sticking my neck out. So just look out for yourself and don't worry about me. I'm still safe."

She paused. "I'm assuming that today's wind-tunnel tests went off all right. So maybe this will be over for us real soon. If not—will you give Tom a hug for me?"

"Sure." A tear slid down Gail's cheek, and the line went dead. She reached over and cradled the receiver.

"What the hell was that all about?" Alex asked.

"Wrong number."

Gail felt him rise onto one elbow, as if to look past her at the telephone. "Chatty son of a gun, wasn't he?"

She sat up, suddenly aware of her nakedness. She had been a fool to think she could counterfeit a night of passion with Alex and not have it fly back into her face.

Alex tried to draw her down next to him. Gail jerked away with a sob and darted to the bathroom, hearing him call out to her as she slammed the door.

Alone in the pitch darkness, her feet braced on the cold tiles, she leaned against the door and succumbed to silent, racking sobs. How quickly her world had been turned inside out, leaving her emotions raw and exposed to the pitiless consequences of her own deceit.

A faint scratching penetrated her consciousness, along with the sound of his concerned voice. "Darling?"

The doorknob rattled slightly as he turned it. Alex pushed open the door against Gail's yielding weight. She backed away, bumping into the cold porcelain sink.

"What is it, darling?" Alex asked, taking her into his arms. When her tears touched his bare chest, she felt his pectoral muscles tighten, but he said nothing.

After awhile he led her back to bed, where he held her in the crook of his body, stroking her and mur-

muring soothing words that she barely heard. Gail was aware only of a band of excruciating pain around her heart.

GAIL AWOKE in the night to find herself curled snugly against Alex's chest. She could tell from his slow, steady breathing that he was sound asleep. But his arms were locked around her, as if he were trying to protect her from something.

She lay very still, sketchily recalling how he had allowed her to cry herself to sleep, no questions asked. Her pain returned with full force, but not the tears. In their place she felt a vague fear and the dread of impending loneliness.

The phone on the night table rang loudly. Alex bolted awake, entangling them both in the bedclothes.

"Damnation!" he muttered. "What now?"

He reached for the telephone, knocked it off the night table, and leaned over the side of the bed to grope for it on the floor. Finding it, he thrust the receiver into Gail's hand.

"Monica?" Adelaide's voice rasped into Gail's ear. "Sorry to wake you, but something's happened out at Monarch. Tom's been trying to reach Alex, but he doesn't answer at his apartment. Do you have any idea where he is?"

"No," Gail said automatically. "But I'll track him down and pass along the message. What's going on?"

"Just tell him it's the worst kind of emergency," Adelaide replied and hung up.

"Track who down?" Alex asked.

"You." Gail was starkly awake now, adrenaline pulsing through her veins. In the aftermath of the alarming call, she had an uneasy feeling that Adelaide knew exactly where Alex was. "Tom needs you at Monarch. Some kind of emergency."

Gail started to get up, but Alex pressed her back against the pillow. "You need the rest," he said. "I'll call you if we need you."

He rushed into the bathroom and turned on the light. She heard him hurriedly splashing water into his face. Then he was back in the bedroom, sorting his clothes from hers in the shaft of light from the bathroom.

Gail sat up in bed, the sheet pulled high under her arms, watching him dress hastily. When he had his pants and shoes on, he came and knelt on the edge of the bed.

"Sweetheart, I don't know what upset you tonight," he said with an urgent intensity. "But if you can hang on just a little while longer, we'll work it out together, no matter what. I already know I can't live without you."

He kissed her, then embraced her quickly, his beard stubble raking her cheek. Before Gail could find her voice, Alex had grabbed his shirt and coat and left the room. Seconds later, she heard the front door close.

She sat stunned, the taste of his kiss lingering on her lips. She tried to imagine how he would react when he learned that she was not Monica, but quickly turned away from the thought. She would cross that bridge of pain when she came to it.

Somehow she would manage to close the door on this night. If there were rough times ahead when loneliness became unbearable, then perhaps she could reopen that door and peek at the treasured moments of passion she had shared with the one true love of her life. But not now.

Gail shook herself, stiffening her chin with determination. This was no time to be wallowing in melodramatic self-pity. She had stepped into this hornet's nest with her eyes wide open, both as a scientist and as a woman. It was time she started behaving like an intelligent human being again.

She shifted her thoughts to Monarch Space Center and swung her feet over the side of the bed. Pulling clothes from the closet, she wondered what kind of emergency Tom had run into.

THE RAIN HAD STOPPED. Shredded clouds raced across the crescent moon as Gail hurried along the apartment complex's sidewalk toward the parking lot. She wished now that Alex had waited for her. The lot was packed with cars, but no people, and the eerie stillness made her skin crawl. Gail shivered in the damp air and approached the Porsche, keys in hand.

She passed a dark, dusty Mazda sedan with a large crack in the windshield. The car didn't seem to belong in these rows of expensive, well-maintained vehicles. She eyed it with suspicion, got into the Porsche and locked the doors.

Gail pulled out of the lot into the cul de sac, accelerating, her mind already shifting ahead to Monarch. She was halfway through town, waiting impatiently at a red traffic light, when she noticed a set of headlights on the deserted street behind her.

She watched them slowly move toward her. The driver couldn't be doing more than ten miles an hour, she thought. Then she realized that she had sat clear through the green light. Flooring the accelerator, she gunned the Porsche through the amber.

Her gaze shot back to the rearview mirror as she heard a squeal of tires behind her. The nocturnal Sunday driver had suddenly come alive and was tearing through the red light.

Gail exhaled sharply, a cold rush of fear clamping her fists around the padded steering wheel. She took the next corner to the right without braking, hardly aware of what she was doing, responding only to a primal urge to flee.

The Porsche hugged the corner in spite of the wet pavement. A quick glance in the side mirror revealed headlights sweeping widely through the turn. Gail moaned at the confirmation that she was indeed being followed. *Chased.*

She took the next left, again without slowing, sped along a sleeping residential street, then shifted smoothly down into one more left turn. Years of driving on Southern California's freeways had given her confidence behind the wheel, and the gutsy performance of Monica's Porsche only enhanced that confidence.

The headlights trailed farther behind with each successive turn, following the Porsche's crisp maneuvers with tortured, roundhouse turns punctuated by the sound of screaming rubber.

Gail took a hard right at the next corner, returning to the street from which she had started. She floored the accelerator once again, praying in vain for a police car. She had almost placed a full block between herself and her pursuer when as she watched in the rearview mirror, it took the corner too fast, spun out, and slammed into a lamppost. She uttered a triumphant cry and sped on toward the highway leading to Monarch.

By the time she reached the road leading into the center, Gail had overcome a severe case of the shakes. She was beginning to think she could master anything. The frightening four-wheel victory had left her with a much-needed sense of control—until she once again began to think about what she was doing, and why she was here.

She checked through the front security gate, a sense of safety encompassing her. Whoever had followed her through town would not get past the white frame kiosk. At least she would be safe while on Monarch's grounds.

Gail worked at composing herself as she rode the elevator up to the Shadow project offices on the second floor. She couldn't be more than ten minutes behind Alex, in spite of the terrifying incident in town. She had dressed like a madwoman and probably looked it, she thought, clawing her fingers through her hair.

After a brief search, she found Tom and Alex in Adelaide's office. They were standing just outside the open door to the Confidential Data room, Tom's hand on Alex's shoulder. Both men glanced up as she entered, their faces drawn.

She took some comfort from the way they stood together, showing none of their earlier animosity. Their private discussion late the previous day seemed to have cleared the air between them. From the way things looked, however, the emergency was every bit as bad as Adelaide had indicated on the phone.

"What's happened?" Gail asked.

"The floppy disk containing the data for the drone's new component package has been stolen," Alex told her.

"Are you sure it wasn't just misplaced?" Gail felt the skin prickling at the back of her neck. Another theft, she thought. Another glaring breach of Shadow's supposedly airtight security.

"Yes," Tom said. "Whoever took it slipped this disk containing garbage into its place." He snatched a floppy disk off Dorie's desk and sent it sailing across the room.

Adelaide appeared in the CD room doorway, grim-faced and angry. "I can't believe this has happened," she said.

Alex looked at her, and Adelaide defiantly drew back her shoulders. "I've never left the CD room door unlocked while I stepped out of this office for even a second, Alex."

"What about the duplicate disk?" Gail wanted to know.

"It's still in the vault," Adelaide replied. "But Alex gave me additional data for the master disk later yesterday, and I didn't get around to updating the duplicate."

"Then you'd better get on that." Alex started for the door.

"I'll call Dorie," Adelaide said.

"No." Alex paused at the door, frowning. He exchanged a brief glance with Tom. "No, maybe you'd better not do that."

Alex jerked open the door and strode out. Gail followed, catching up with him in the corridor.

"You still think Dorie is involved in the thefts and sabotage, don't you?" she asked, almost trotting to keep up with him.

"I think Adelaide isn't as conscientious about keeping the Confidential Data room locked as she likes to believe." Alex shoved open the door to his office. "Maybe Dorie had access to that disk. She could have come back last night. I don't know."

He reached for his telephone. "But I'm going to call Security and find out."

Gail placed a restraining hand upon Alex's arm and felt the muscles leap at her touch. "What does this do to the scheduled wind-tunnel test?" she asked, forcing her thoughts away from the disturbing awareness of the body beneath the rumpled clothes.

"Nothing. But if that component data gets loose, and turns up in foreign hands, we might all be under federal investigation, and the whole project goes down the tubes."

The phone warbled under his hand. He picked it up, and Gail watched his expression go from grim to startled as he spoke in terse monosyllables. Then he hung up and slumped into his desk chair, looking as if the wind had been knocked out of him.

"What is it?" she asked, astounded by the rapid change.

"That was the hospital," he said. "They're looking for Dorie's next of kin."

A chill washed over Gail.

"She's in Intensive Care," Alex went on. "She was found bludgeoned outside her apartment. They think she'll make it, but she's in bad shape."

"Who would do something like that?" Gail leaned heavily against the desk.

"How about Joe? The police indicated Dorie was last seen in Joe's company." Alex looked up at her, his lips a bitter line, one fist clenching the chair arm. "I think this pretty well proves that he must have been using her. Once she gave him what he was after—that disk—he tried to kill her to cover his tracks."

Gail couldn't bring herself to look at Alex. In spite of what Alex was implying, she felt suddenly close to Dorie. She knew what it was like to fall in love with a man and become entrapped by her own weakness.

"Maybe I'd better go be with Dorie," she suggested, pushing away from the desk.

Alex reached for her, but she dodged his hand and hurried toward the door. "Dorie can't have visitors," he told her. "At the moment, Tom might need you more."

Gail turned at the door, as if an invisible tether had yanked her around. Alex noticed how pale she was and saw the haunted vulnerability in her smoky eyes. He wanted to go to her, to fold his arms protectively around the reality of his dream.

Before he could move, she was gone. Alex sat motionless, feeling a sudden emptiness in the room. Gail was more than the living embodiment of his portrait of Monica. Painfully recalling how she had apparently snapped under the stress of her double role and wept herself to sleep, he realized that she had become a vital part of him.

IT WAS JUST AFTER NOON. Gail sat wedged between Tom and Alex in the small electric cart. Tom's left arm stretched across the back of the narrow seat, hanging on as Alex piloted them toward the wind tunnel.

Gail shot furtive glances at Tom. The casual familiarity he had shown toward her over the past several days was missing. So was the aura of friction that had surrounded the three of them whenever they were together. The change puzzled her.

"Thomas, we still haven't spotted that fox in our henhouse," Alex said, his expression impenetrable.

"I've racked my brain," Tom told him. "Joe was on the outside, and Dorie didn't have direct access to the drone model. She could have stolen the disk, but she couldn't have played games in the wind tunnel."

"Right. We have a third party to worry about." Alex scowled, visibly concentrating on the problem. The cart began jigging erratically to and fro. "How does Walt strike you?"

Gail felt Tom tense against her. "Walt's the best man I've got, Alex."

"And he has full access to the drone model," she pointed out.

"So do half a dozen other technicians and about two dozen government and military personnel," Tom said.

Alex's eyes widened, then narrowed. He said nothing and they rode the rest of the way in silence.

Gail reached over almost reflexively a couple of times to adjust Alex's steering. She was aware that Tom was watching her and smiled at him uncertainly. He smiled back, with an odd twist of his lips.

Wedged between the two men, Gail squirmed on the seat. She couldn't tell if the strange absence of friction between Tom and Alex signaled good or bad news for Monica.

They clambered out of the cart in front of the wind-tunnel building. The two big engineers continued to bracket Gail as they entered, heading toward the drone model.

She hooked one arm through Tom's, her thoughts straying again to Monica and Dorie. Monica had chosen correctly, Dorie had apparently made the wrong choice and Gail had had no right to choose at all. Her deception had made her a nonperson. She removed her arm from Tom's and shivered, feeling a sudden chill envelop her. Tom moved closer, placing a protective arm around her shoulders.

CHAPTER THIRTEEN

INSIDE THE WIND TUNNEL a uniformed sentry stood guard over a box on the floor. Alex ordered him out of the tunnel, along with several other workers. As the lab-coated technicians filed out, Tom picked up the box and carried it to the drone.

"You've certainly had a change of attitude about installing this," Gail observed. She held the foam-cushioned metal box, while Tom lifted out the Shadow drone model's last-minute component package. Some distance away, Alex was securing the wind-tunnel door from the inside.

Tom smiled crookedly at her. "Alex finally told me what this little gem does," he said. "That helped."

"It doesn't look like much, does it?" Gail commented.

He held up the small, oblong device. Short tentacles of wiring protruded stiffly from two sides. The lightweight metal casing carried no markings or identification of any kind.

"Looks can be deceiving," Alex said, coming up behind Tom.

Tom gave him a sidelong glance and replied, "Yeah. Tell me about it."

Alex raised one eyebrow. He glanced at Gail, and she felt her skin flush hotly. For an instant she felt his hands on the soft curves and valleys of her body. Something in the warm probing of his eyes told her that she was not alone in her thoughts.

Gail didn't find that comforting, especially when she realized that Tom had observed the intimate way Alex was eyeing her. She couldn't believe Alex had the nerve to flaunt his feelings for Monica in front of his best friend.

"Let's get this baby installed before Walt storms the ramparts," Tom suggested curtly.

She peeked over his shoulder toward the observation points. Walt and a double row of technicians stood outside the tunnel, watching their every move, looking none too happy. Alex had taken extraordinary security measures in deciding that Tom should install the highly classified new component himself, and the technicians were clearly taking it as a personal insult.

"Alex, if you're wrong about Walt being the one who stole the sensor unit and sabotaged the first test, he's never going to forgive you for being so distrustful of him," Gail pointed out.

She spoke in an undertone, even though the wind-tunnel door was closed and the technicians outside the windows probably couldn't hear a word.

"True." Alex lifted the panel from the side of the drone model and watched Tom insert the component. "On the other hand, if I'm right, I won't care what he thinks."

Thinking of the night she had just spent with him in the role of his best friend's fiancée, Gail couldn't help wondering if Alex really cared what anybody thought about his actions. The farther she got from the blinding emotions of those hours, the guiltier she felt. In Tom's presence she had grown as remorseful as if she actually were Monica.

"She has a point, Alex," Tom commented, frowning as he made a delicate wiring connection.

Alex swapped Tom a screwdriver for the pliers he was holding, slapping the tool into his hand like a surgeon's assistant. Gail watched how well the two men worked together and felt a twinge of real anger toward Alex. His ability to so blithely deceive Tom far exceeded her own nerve-racking efforts at flimflamming.

"You don't understand the half of it, bucko," Alex said.

Tom twisted his head around to squint at Alex. "Meaning?"

"Later." Alex smiled enigmatically. "Do you have that blue wire crimped properly?"

"Certainly."

Gail backed away from the drone, icy hands clenched inside her lab-coat pockets. *Later,* he had said. Would Alex really be so unfeeling as to tell Tom how he felt about Monica? Gail shuddered at the thought.

Remembering how he had held her so tenderly, she couldn't believe that Alex could be so lacking in human decency. And yet he had made love to her last night, believing her to be Monica, hadn't he? If he could do that behind his best friend's back, how much decency could he have?

Alex's peripheral vision detected movement and he glanced toward Gail. She was backing toward the wind-tunnel door, her gaze riveted on him. Her expression sent a chill through him. Leaving Tom to finish on the drone, he started toward her.

"What's the problem?" he asked.

Gail had stopped at the door, her hand on the latch. She wasn't exactly sure. It was all tangled up in the confusion of duplicity and lies that her life had become.

"You, Alex," she said, and a sharp pain skewered her as she recognized the truth of that. "You are the problem."

"I don't understand." He spread his hands to emphasize his words.

"Later," she said, mimicking him sardonically as tears ached at the backs of her eyes. "You don't know the half of it, bucko."

She started to open the door, but he grabbed her arm and whirled her around. Gail looked up at him, breathlessly aware of his towering strength.

"This isn't the time to play games," he told her, his voice too low to carry back to Tom. "I want to know what you're thinking *right now*."

"I think you're probably the most insensitive human being on the face of the earth," she whispered hoarsely, wrenching her arm free. "How can you go to bed with your best friend's fiancée and then turn right around and act as if nothing happened? Worse, you treat it like a joke."

Alex rocked back on his heels as if she had struck him. And Gail *wanted* to hit him—to make him hurt as much as she was hurting now.

"Is success all that matters to you, Alex?" Gail demanded, barely able to keep her voice down. "Don't you care about anybody or anything besides that blasted drone?"

"I care about you," he said harshly.

Gail stared at him in disbelief. "And what about Tom?" she snapped. "Have you no consideration at all for him?"

"Dammit, of course I do." Alex rubbed hard at the back of his neck. "I'd walk through fire for both of you."

"Talk is cheap." Almost insane, Gail rummaged through the rubble of the past few days, searching for something heavy to fling at him. "If you're so all-fired caring about our welfare, then why did Adelaide tell me you wouldn't want me to call the police when my apartment was broken into?"

His jaw slid to one side, and Gail glared at him, seeing that she had hit him hard. She felt a rush of double-edged satisfaction in having successfully wounded someone she loved.

She waited for him to sling barbed words at her, to try to hurt her back. She wanted to be hurt deeper, so she would no longer have the capacity to love Alex Shepard. She wanted him to kill everything she had ever felt for him—right here, right now. Because she didn't want to love a man who cared only when it suited his purpose.

But he stood mute before her, unmoving, as if in a state of suspended animation. If he were behind the wheel of the electric cart, she thought irrelevantly, he could be heading straight for a brick wall and not see it. She realized with a crushing certainty that he was not even seeing her.

"I wish I had never set eyes on you, Alex," Gail said, almost choking on the words. "I really do."

Through a blur of pain, she saw Tom start toward them as Alex reached for her. She jerked on the door latch, shrinking from both of them, and stumbled out of the wind tunnel as the door flew open.

"Monica!"

Her sister's name echoed after her in Tom's voice as Gail ran through the cavernous building, feeling as if she were falling, falling into a bottomless black hole.

GAIL PACED CIRCLES around the electric cart, feeling washed out. The afternoon had dragged by, and the evening was crawling along in slow motion. She had moved through the past dozen hours as if drugged, thinking and feeling no more than absolutely necessary to get by.

She had spent a couple of hours at the hospital, rooted to a hard plastic chair outside Intensive Care. She had gotten to see Dorie twice, for five minutes. The second time, Dorie had awakened enough to squeeze her hand weakly.

They had silently cried together—both of them shedding bitter tears for their folly, Gail thought. But the tears hadn't helped. At the hospital, then back at Monarch, where she had returned late in the afternoon, Gail had continued to carry Alex Shepard around with her like an open chest wound.

"Hop in, Monica. We're off!"

Gail stopped pacing as Adelaide came huffing up to the electric cart, clutching a fistful of floppy disks. Gail climbed in, grateful for any distraction that would even temporarily get her mind off the personal disaster that she had brought upon herself.

"Hold on to these, Monica." Adelaide handed her the disks. "Alex wants me and the software to be front and center during the test, in case there are any glitches in the computer-controlled functions."

As Adelaide aimed the cart toward the wind-tunnel building, it occurred to Gail that Alex drove the machine like an afterthought, while Adelaide manhandled it like the commander of a Sherman tank. At least she kept to the roadway and didn't play chicken with inanimate objects, Gail reflected.

They were just leaving the parking area adjoining the main office building, when Gail gasped and turned in the seat, nearly dropping the floppy disks. A dark, dusty car was backed into an unreserved slot near the edge of the lot. She spotted the cracked windshield first, then the crumpled right fender with the smashed right headlight. Before Gail could register more than the original shock wave, they had passed the car and were humming speedily toward the wind-tunnel building.

"Something's been bugging you all afternoon," Adelaide said with her usual blunt impatience. "What gives?"

Gail straightened in the seat, dry-mouthed, instinctively trying to cover for herself. "I've been worried about Dorie," she said, clinging to the half truth.

She didn't want to have to explain the car. Nor could she tell Adelaide that she had dropped the ball as Monica's stand-in. Tom and Monica—Alex and Monica. The juggling act had finally gotten out of hand, leaving Monica and her unborn child out in the cold, at the mercy of men who stalked their prey on lonely streets at night. A wintery hollowness lingered in the pit of Gail's stomach.

"Well, we need to have our heads up for this last test," Adelaide said stiffly. "There'll be plenty of time to fret over Dorie tomorrow."

Gail blinked, realizing that Adelaide's nerves were stretched trigger taut. She studied the older woman's face in the flashing glow from the security lights as they sped toward the wind tunnel.

Adelaide was sort of a basic, hard-nosed version of Alex, she thought, but without the unpredictable splashes of color that his artist's personality presented—and without the tenderness.

Tom was waiting for them outside the wind-tunnel building. He held a small box tucked under one arm. Adelaide got out and breezed past him into the building with hardly a word.

He held out a hand to Gail, smiling. She looked up into his black eyes as she stepped from the cart. He seemed less tense than she had expected. The way his hand lingered on hers gave Gail a small quiver of renewed hope for Monica. Raising her chin, however, he gave her a distinctly brotherly kiss on the forehead.

When she looked at him curiously, he chuckled and handed her the box. "Alex asked me to give you this," he said. "After you dressed him down in the wind tunnel this afternoon, he seemed to think a peace offering was in order."

Gail raised the flap on the box and peered in at two perfect, blush-orange peaches nestled in green tissue paper. "Peaches?"

Tom shook his head, still smiling. "Alex has been acting a trifle weird lately."

"Weird isn't the word for it," she murmured, as they entered the building and headed for the control center. "Peaches. Why, do you think?"

"I'm just beginning to get a very fuzzy picture," Tom said, wobbling a hand from side to side. "Why don't you ask him?"

Alex emerged from a cluster of air force observers and lab-coated technicians near the control center and came striding toward Tom and Gail. He grinned at the open box that Gail held in both hands like a time bomb.

"They're imported," he said.

"Where from?" Tom asked.

"I don't know. I guess that's what intrigued me about them." Alex clasped his hands behind his back, looking self-satisfied.

Tom plucked one of the peaches from the box. "Smells good enough to eat," he said, taking a bite.

"That's the spirit, Thomas!" Alex took the second peach from the box and rolled it in his hand. "Soft, sweet, succulent. I thought about saving them for a still life, but some things just can't be captured in paint."

He winked at Gail. Then he threw an arm around Tom's shoulders and they walked off toward the control center.

Gail stood flat-footed, staring down into the empty box. "It's me," she said, under her breath. "I'm losing my mind."

Tom stopped at the edge of the control center crowd and waited for her. By the time she caught up, all he had left was the peach pit. He dropped it into the box and closed the lid.

"How about a kiss for luck?" he suggested, checking his watch.

Gail smiled and stood on tiptoe to peck him on the lips, grateful that he still wanted this from Monica. "You don't need luck, Tom."

"I hope you're right."

Tom looked at her searchingly. For just an instant, a glimmer of fear hovered in his eyes. Then he turned and walked briskly toward the control center.

Gail started to follow, but stopped. Beyond a cluster of military observers she thought she glimpsed Dick Brady. She moved in that direction, but before she could reach the point where he had been standing, he had disappeared. She turned in a slow circle, wondering if she had only imagined the NSA officer being there.

Glancing at her watch, Gail shoved Dick Brady from her thoughts and began wending her way back through the crowd toward Tom. She was halfway to the control center, when she pulled up short.

She had almost run head-on into Alex and Howard Eastman, walking arm in arm. They were so caught up in what appeared to be a guarded conversation that neither man noticed her. Gail watched, puzzled, until Eastman patted Alex on the back and they parted company.

Just before Eastman, too, vanished into the crowd, she experienced a sudden jolt of déjà vu. Eastman ducked his head, and she realized that he was the man she had glimpsed inside the pickup truck on the highway outside Pinehaven last Friday. He was minus the beard and slouch hat, but now she understood why she had suddenly braked as she pulled around the truck after asking directions of the man with the crooked eye.

Confused and more than a little frightened, she moved on to the control center, where she only half listened to technicians running through the last-minute checklist. She was staring blank-faced into the wind tunnel at the poised Shadow model, when someone grabbed her arm.

"Listen to me," Alex whispered urgently, his hand grasping her upper arm as if with a vise. "Stay close to me during the test. Do you hear?"

Gail looked at him, startled by his hard-edged intensity, and nodded dumbly. Alex released her and turned back to the controls. Gail looked to her right at Tom and found him staring at her. Again she saw the fear shining brightly in his eyes and shuddered.

"Power up." The sound of Tom's voice sent a hush through the crowd. Gail felt the familiar thrum of the giant turbines. She glanced from Tom to Alex. Whatever feelings she had seen on their faces earlier were now masked by concentration.

As the wind velocity rose inside the tunnel, so did her own sense of apprehension. She couldn't keep her mind on the test. Instead she kept glancing over her shoulder, searching the rapt faces behind her for Brady and Eastman.

What was Dick Brady doing there? Had she really seen him? And what about Eastman? Until moments ago, Gail hadn't been aware that Alex knew the military intelligence officer. Yet she had seen them engaged in apparently serious conversation.

Alex brushed against her, and she took a step out of his way, bumping into Adelaide. The woman slapped her with a withering glance. Gail edged farther into the clustered observers, unable to think straight in such close proximity to Alex, Tom and Adelaide.

She bumped into someone else. Walt nudged her back without so much as looking to see who she was, his gaze nailed to the drone model. Gail kept on drifting slowly backward, with an eerie feeling that she was bouncing off dangerous obstacles in an increasingly frightening stretch of river rapids.

Emerging from the crowd, she took a deep breath, as if she had just surfaced from a lengthy dive. But her sense of apprehension remained at a high pitch.

She couldn't see the Shadow at all from where she stood. Spotting a temporary catwalk that had been erected against the far wall, she hurried over and crept up the rubber-treaded steps. From her new vantage point she could see the drone model as well as the entire array of technicians and spectators collected at the observation points.

Adelaide had moved in to take Gail's place next to Alex, with Walt close behind. As far as Gail could tell from that distance, the test was proceeding without a hitch.

Her gaze began to drift across the spectators, standing as motionless as cardboard cutouts, all facing away from her. She was scanning the backs of their heads, searching for Brady or Eastman, when a movement caught her eye.

A man in a dark suit was making his way out of the crowd, just as she had done moments earlier. When he turned slightly in her direction, Gail tensed. He was some distance from her, but not so far away that she didn't notice the crooked eye.

He reached into his pocket and slowly brought out a small object about the size of a cigarette pack. Gail leaned over the catwalk railing, straining to get a better look. When he turned it over in his hand, moving his thumb on the casing, it reminded her fleetingly of a garage-door opener.

Then he raised it in front of him and pointed it toward the wind tunnel—directly toward the Shadow— and Gail suddenly knew exactly what it was.

"No!" she screamed, reaching out with one hand as if to grab him across the impossible distance that separated them. "Stop that man! Stop him!"

She leaped down the steps, taking them two at a time, still screaming. The man seemed to turn toward her in slow motion, his expression reflecting alarm and awakening anger. But his hand still held the signaling device toward the drone model, and as Gail cleared the last step, she knew she could never reach him in time.

CHAPTER FOURTEEN

ALEX SPUN AROUND as the drone responded to a computer command and its internal navigational equipment became active. He heard Gail scream again, then realized that she was no longer standing next to him.

"Get outa my way!" he bellowed, shoving through the spectators hemming him in at the control panel.

The man with the crooked eye crouched, his arm cocked, as Gail rushed at him. He dropped low, preparing to swing at her, and she got a clear look past him—straight at Howard Eastman. The military intelligence officer stood frozen, fear written all over his face.

Gail was two strides from the crooked-eyed man when Alex charged past her, and drove a fist into the man's face. She heard a sickening crunch. The signaling device flew from the man's hand and went skittering across the floor; he reeled but did not go down.

"Get it, Gail!" Alex shouted.

She pounced upon the transmitter, then became aware that the saboteur was now running toward the main entrance. She also saw that Howard Eastman had finally come to life again and seemed to be in hot pursuit.

So Gail was dismayed when she saw Alex spring after Eastman and bring him down with a snarling tackle. They both hit the floor, grappling. Eastman landed a solid punch to Alex's rib cage, appearing to drive the wind out of him. He rolled on top of Alex, pressing a forearm viciously against his throat. Alex bared his teeth, red-faced, clearly straining against Eastman's weight.

Gail looked around desperately. The crowd of spectators had drawn back to give the men room. She spotted Colonel Bryant at the forefront of a wedge of air force uniforms, his mouth gaping, none of his entourage apparently prepared to intervene.

Beyond the military observers she saw only lab coats; the Shadow technicians continued to concentrate on the wind tunnel.

As if events were testing her sanity to the limit, Gail saw Adelaide take a swing at Walt—then go down like a sack of potatoes, when Walt cursed and took a swing of his own. A ragged cheer went up from the wind-tunnel crew.

Alex formed a bridge with his back, heaving Eastman off him. Gail heard Alex cough and gasp for breath, and both men rolled toward the wall, kicking and clawing at each other as if they were the only two people in the building. Neither seemed able to get the upper hand.

On the wall just beyond them, Gail could see a fire hose neatly accordioned behind glass. Above it a sign read: In Case Of Emergency, Break Glass. Without hesitating, Gail ran past them and broke the glass. The fire hose tumbled out at her feet. She grabbed a double handful of the canvas hose, raising the heavy brass nozzle overhead. She hesitated only briefly, then brought the nozzle down upon the back of Eastman's head. He grunted and went limp in Alex's grasp.

Alex shoved him away and with great effort managed to sit up and prop himself against the wall, his chest heaving. He sat there, legs sprawled, licking the bleeding corner of his lip with his tongue and staring up at Gail.

Still holding the fire hose in one hand, her other hand was plastered over her mouth in horror as she looked down at Eastman's inert body. She had just clobbered a government official. Over the babble of loud voices that seemed to surround her, Gail heard in her mind the numbing sound of a Leavenworth Prison cell door clanging shut behind her.

She pried her gaze off Eastman and looked at Alex. He grinned at her, blood trickling down his chin.

"Don't worry," he said. "He's a bad guy."

Her knees suddenly felt wobbly. Gail wanted to go to Alex, but her feet wouldn't move. She realized that the fire hose had slipped from her hand, and that the sound she'd imagined as the cell door had in fact been the brass nozzle striking the floor.

With a tremendous effort she found her voice and said, "You called me Gail."

"Did I?" Alex raked a sleeve of his lab coat across his chin and mouth, but the action didn't wipe away the grin.

The nearby crowd shifted and Dick Brady appeared, dragging the crooked-eyed man in his wake, hands cuffed behind him with a strip of toothed plastic.

"Are you okay, Shepard?" Brady asked, squatting next to Eastman.

"If that uproar over at the control center meant what I think it did," Alex replied, "I'm a whole lot better than okay."

Brady turned Eastman onto his back.

"By the way, I didn't do that to him," Alex said, suddenly serious. "She did." He pointed at Gail.

Brady pursed his lips, and for a moment Gail had a panicky thought that she had been thrown to the wolves. But Brady just shook his head and said, "The woman continues to amaze me."

"Power down!" Tom's elated voice boomed over the crowd with the steely penetration of a drill instructor.

Faces turned toward the wind tunnel, as though the spectators were just now remembering why they were all there. Gail felt the wind turbines winding down. But even when Adelaide appeared in the custody of a uniformed security guard, the beginnings of a shiner already swelling her left eye, Gail couldn't seem to budge.

Her mind was freewheeling, unable to put the scattered pieces of this maniacal puzzle together. Only one thing remained crystal clear.

He called me Gail.

She was still trying to get a handle on that, when Tom pushed his way through a narrow gap in the crowd. He did a double take when he saw Alex propped against the wall, happily bleeding from the mouth, with Howard Eastman, just now regaining consciousness, at his feet. Gail looked at him imploringly, and Tom quickly sidestepped Eastman to put an arm around her.

"Would someone please tell me what the hell's been going on around here?" Tom asked.

Alex took another swipe at his mouth with his coat sleeve and laughed. "Partner, you'd better pull up a chair, because this is going to take awhile."

Gail crawled an arm around Tom for support and looked down at Alex's jaunty grin. She too felt as if she were on the outside, looking in.

THE CRESCENT MOON hung just over the tops of the pines that bordered the Monarch facility. Gail stood alone on the sidewalk outside the entrance to the wind-tunnel building, looking into the starry sky as she hugged herself in the chilly night air. She had lost all track of time.

Three government cars wheeled across the nearly emptied parking lot in front of her, heading single file toward the distant front gate. The grimness of what had taken place earlier came home to Gail as she made out the figures of Adelaide and Eastman seated behind the wire-mesh screen in the middle car.

The vehicles passed directly beneath a security light, and Gail thought she saw Adelaide's head turn her way, just before the cars sped up and disappeared around a building.

The door behind her opened and closed, and footsteps approached on the pavement. A hand settled companionably upon her shoulder. She knew without looking that it was Tom's. He had only rarely lost body contact with her since the successful Shadow test had been completed.

"Why would a woman like Adelaide gamble away everything that way?" she asked quietly, grateful for

Tom's company. Now that the madness had ended, she was beginning to feel terribly alone.

"Greed," Dick Brady said from behind Tom. "Double-dip greed, at that. On one hand Adelaide was selling Shadow's software to Weissman Aircraft—and on the other she was trying to pass key hardware from some of the components to foreign interests through Eastman."

Gail turned. "She stole the floppy disk herself? And the part from the sensor unit?"

"She stole the disk," Brady told her. "But Eastman had some bad guys on his back, pushing him hard for that sensor-unit part. He made that switch himself, not knowing that Adelaide had placed the explosive charge to delay or even kill the Shadow project, giving Weissman a clear field."

"Eastman could get into the wind tunnel to do that?" Gail asked.

"That was my fault," Tom admitted. "Walt knew Eastman was in government intelligence, and so he assumed Eastman had security clearance for access to the drone model. I should have caught that."

"You should have?" Brady laughed harshly. "What about me? I've been working with Eastman for months, and it never entered my mind that he had gone over to the other side. Alex finally made the connection this evening, when Tom mentioned that government personnel had access to the drone model.

Since Eastman also had inside information about the investigation, he seemed a likely candidate. Alex and I talked it over and decided to let the test proceed in hopes that Eastman would reveal his hand. Thanks to Adelaide and her hired klutz, we now have more than just circumstantial evidence."

Gail recalled the "holes" she had noticed in Monica's project game book. Obviously Eastman had been the one who tampered with it.

"Tom, is Walt still ticked off at Alex for suspecting him?" she inquired.

"Very. And the way Walt holds grudges, he'll probably chew on it until he comes up with a suitable method of revenge."

They turned as Alex came out of the building and ambled down the sidewalk to join them. Gail noticed that he held one arm across his midsection, nursing his bruised ribs, but was nonetheless smiling. He hadn't stopped smiling since the brawl.

"How did you finally get on to Adelaide?" Tom asked, pulling Gail a little closer.

"That was Gail's doing," Alex answered for Brady. He cupped a hand gently around the back of her neck.

"Mine?" Gail looked up at him, puzzled.

"Sure. When you blew up at me in the wind tunnel, you said Adelaide had told you that I wouldn't want you to call the police after your—after Monica's apartment was broken into. The truth was, Adelaide had left me with the impression that the police had already been notified."

"Naturally Adelaide wouldn't want the police nosing around," Brady added. "Especially since the intruder was working for her."

"Who was the intruder?" Gail wanted to know, aware that Alex was applying pressure with the hand he'd placed on her neck, trying to draw her closer. But Tom held on to her just as firmly on his side.

"The daffy-eyed klutz with the signaling device," Brady said, pulling out a pack of cigarettes and offering them around. Both Alex and Tom squeezed her when Gail declined.

"Adelaide wasn't exactly on the inside track when it came to hiring muscle," Brady continued, lighting up. "According to her, he fouled up at every turn. The day you first spotted him near Pinehaven, Gail, he was supposed to abduct Alex, the way he had Monica."

Tom tensed. "What about...?"

"But he panicked and tried to bash my brains out instead?" Alex asked, his hand going to his forehead.

"It seems so." Brady took a long drag on his cigarette and blew the smoke into the night breeze. "After that, he practically made a spectacle of himself when he broke into Monica's place, looking for the

Shadow sketch. And then he blew it as a hit man when Adelaide and Eastman sent him after Dorie.''

"Adelaide?" Gail questioned. "What about Joe?"

Brady shook his head. "Joe Anderson works for me."

"You're kidding. Then Dorie never passed him anything?"

"As a matter of fact, she did." Brady shook his head again and flipped his cigarette butt across the sidewalk. "Joe kept pressing her for Shadow information, so she gave him a floppy disk the afternoon before she was attacked.

"Joe hightailed it directly to me with it. I was meeting with Eastman at the time. Eastman must have figured that since Dorie was getting into the classified-data-leaking business herself, he could help keep us off Adelaide's trail by having Dorie taken out."

"What was on that disk?" Alex asked.

Brady sighed. "Dorie's 1986 income tax return. It seems that she was testing Joe with it. If he took it from her purse—which he did—she intended to report him."

"I'll be damned," Alex said softly.

"Yeah. Joe feels pretty bad about the whole thing. He's been at the hospital with her the entire time, except when one of you showed up."

"You want to know what *I* feel bad about?" Tom asked. "I'm the only one here who seems the least bit concerned about what's happened to Monica!"

"I care," Gail said, suddenly aware of Tom's lightly reined anger. "And you're right, Tom. I'm tired of waiting, too."

"I've told both of you that Monica is fine," Brady said. "She finally made contact with her field control agent a couple of days ago. We had a very enlightening conversation this afternoon. Why don't we mosey on over to the Shadow offices, and I'll make a couple of calls."

Alex started toward the electric cart that Adelaide had left parked near the curb. Gail pulled him up short.

"I've had enough excitement for one night, Alex," she said, steering him along the walkway. "How about if we just go on foot?"

"Amen to that," Tom agreed. "It would be kind of pathetic to have made it through all this, just to have Alex cream us against a dumpster."

"What are you talking about?" Alex protested, but walked along with them, anyway. He wasn't about to let go of Gail.

"Speaking of driving," Brady added, bringing up the rear, "who taught you, Gail? Barney Oldfield? Mario Andretti?"

Gail looked questioningly over her shoulder.

"You ran me a merry chase on your way over here from your apartment this evening," Brady told her, scowling. "I'm still trying to figure out how to get a new headlight and fender on my NSA expense account."

"That was you?" Gail gaped at him. She would have stopped, but Tom and Alex dragged her along between them.

"After what happened to Dorie, I thought I'd better keep a closer eye on you," Brady said. "I had no idea you were this capable of taking care of yourself."

Gail faced front again, her thoughts swimming. Very little had been what it seemed, these past several days. She was having trouble sorting out what was real and what wasn't.

"By the way, Shepard," Brady added, "you put on quite a show for Colonel Bryant tonight."

"Yeah," Alex said sardonically. "I was thinking about bringing in a bunch of mud wrestlers, but thought that might be too flashy."

"I believe Brady is talking about Shadow's test," Tom observed.

"Oh, that old thing," Alex drawled, then laughed. "Bryant underwent a substantial attitude adjustment when he found out Weissman Aircraft was going to be taken out of the running by the long arm of the law."

"Bryant crawfished," Gail said simply.

"He'll be standing at your door with his brass hat in his hand tomorrow," Brady assured Alex.

"I won't be there," Alex replied. "The Shadow team—what's left of it—is taking the day off."

He slipped his arm around Gail's waist and tightened his hold on her. For a moment something deep within her leaped. Then her uncertainty about him returned to haunt her. *Had* he thought he was making love to Monica last night?

"What a night!" Alex said exuberantly, looking up at the moon.

He tried again to pull Gail closer. Again he met with Tom's stubborn resistance.

"Come on, man," he said, grinning over her head at Tom. "Let go of her. They're a matched set, all right. But this one's mine."

Tom looked back at him humorlessly. "Forget it. I'll swap even stephen for Monica, period. Until then, you can consider me Gail's Siamese twin."

They entered the foyer of the Monarch Building three abreast, hurrying Gail along between them. She was beginning to feel like a hostage.

"Wait!" she demanded as they stepped into the elevator.

Brady paused with his finger over the floor button. Tom and Alex both loosened their hold on her slightly. She looked from one engineer to the other.

Alex appeared almost drunk with humor, his amber eyes shocking her with their brilliance. Tom looked anxious.

"Exactly how long have you two known I wasn't Monica?" she asked, half-afraid of their answer.

"I had a feeling something wasn't right, back at Pinehaven," Tom told her. "But it really didn't occur to me that you weren't Monica until I took you home after dinner the other night."

"Oh, come on, Thomas," Alex said, jabbing Tom's shoulder. "I've dropped enough hints."

"Shut up and let Tom finish!" Gail felt as if she were dangling at the end of her rope.

"I couldn't make any sense at all of your *hints,* Alex," Tom went on. "Not until I noticed that her ears weren't pierced."

"Ears?" Alex cupped a hand over Gail's ear and pulled her head against his chest. "What were you doing with Gail's ears, man?"

"I thought they were Monica's," Tom said through his teeth.

Gail pulled herself away from Alex, growing exasperated with his high spirits. "When did *you* know, Alex?"

"From the very beginning," Alex said smugly.

"Not quite," Brady corrected him, punching the floor button. "He got suspicious Sunday night, Gail. I had to tell him about you then."

Gail felt herself sway as the elevator started up. "He's known since Sunday night?"

Brady nodded. She shifted her gaze to Alex, remembering his tenderness and passion one night ago, and something inside her took wing. The warmth in his eyes deepened. Gail was beginning to think he was going to bend and kiss her right there in front of Tom and Brady, when the elevator door glided open.

They stepped out at the second floor. Gail moved like a sleepwalker, barely aware of her surroundings. At the door to the Shadow project offices, Alex slipped his code card into the lock.

"I'm not Monica!" she exclaimed suddenly, as Tom opened the door.

All three men raised their eyebrows.

"I don't have to go in there anymore," she went on, balking as Brady tried to usher the three of them through the doorway. "And I'm not going to. I've had my fill of this place."

Gail turned on Brady. "I want to know where my sister is."

She was suddenly obsessed with the need to be with Monica. Now they were equals—equals in looks and equals in love. They were two separate people, yet were both parts of the same whole. She wanted that other part of herself.

"I'm leaving here this minute, Dick Brady," she said, pointing back toward the elevator. "You tell me where Monica is."

Brady raised his head and eyed her sternly. "Why don't we just go on inside and have a cup of coffee, while I make a couple of phone calls?" he proposed, as if talking to a rebellious child.

"Gail's right, Brady," Tom said. "Where the hell's Monica?"

Brady never took his gaze from Gail. And suddenly she knew, saw it in the hint of a smile that he fought to conceal. She turned and bolted through the door past Tom and Alex.

Then she was in Alex's office, locked in Monica's tearful embrace. "You're safe!" Gail exclaimed over and over in a choked voice. For a timeless moment they clung to each other, children again in their hearts. When they finally drew apart, Gail felt as if her center of gravity had somehow shifted to a point between them—a point that Monica shared.

"I'll be damned."

They turned in unison at the sound of Tom's voice. Monica sucked in her breath.

"I'll be double-damned," Tom said wonderingly, standing in the doorway. "Would you look at that?"

"I'm looking," said Alex. Seeing the two women together for the first time was indeed a staggering experience.

"It's like an optical illusion, isn't it?" Brady added.

"I just had a horrible thought," Alex resumed. "What if Gail gets her ears pierced? How will we be able to tell them apart?"

"That's my job," Tom affirmed.

"How so?"

"I've kissed them both, old buddy. I could tell them apart in a blackout."

Tom moved toward Monica, arms outstretched. She rushed into them, he lifted her and whirled her around with a roar.

"Easy, Tommy!" Monica laughed. "You'll make us dizzy!"

Tom almost dropped her. "Us?"

She hung from his neck, smiling coyly. "Us."

"Oh, my God!" he breathed, setting her down gently and holding her by the shoulders.

Gail watched them share a moment of purest silence. When Tom pulled Monica to him and kissed her with deep tenderness, Gail felt tears run down her cheeks.

She leaned back and closed her eyes, enormously relieved that Tom and Monica's relationship had survived. Then Gail straightened suddenly and spun around, to find herself in Alex's arms. She had been so caught up in Tom and Monica's reunion that she hadn't realized that Alex had come up behind her, and that she had been lolling against his chest.

"I never have thanked you for lowering the boom on Eastman," he said, his fingers locked behind her back so that she stood very close to him. Alex bent and lightly kissed the corner of one tear-filled eye.

"No need to thank me," she said, fully sharing his sense of elation now. "It's a service I provide for men I'm crazy about."

"Men?"

"Special men."

"Are there many?"

She smiled. "Only one, so far. I'm very choosy."

"This one man," Alex said, kissing the corner of her other eye. "Can you see him being a part of your life—permanently?"

Gail wrapped her arms around him carefully, mindful of his bruised ribs. "Oh, yes," she said, floating. "He's the sort of fellow who needs someone at his side at all times, to watch out for trees."

A door closed softly behind them. Alex's eyes darted to one side, leaving hers for just an instant. Gail was glad that Brady hadn't made a production of leaving.

"I ought to thank Brady, too," Alex went on. "For sending you here."

"So what's there to thank him for?" Gail inquired doubtfully. "He could have just introduced us at a seminar or something."

Alex kissed her between the eyes. "I'm not sure that would have been the same."

He lifted her chin and pressed his lips to hers. His cut lip made him wince slightly. But not even the pain could prevent him from kissing Gail now.

CHAPTER FIFTEEN

BRIGHT, late-November sunlight glinted through the bubble canopy of the small Bell helicopter, making Gail's eyes water. She tightened her seat belt apprehensively as the rotor began turning.

Alex spoke briefly into his head set, while the helicopter rested lightly on its skids. Then she watched his hands move surely over the controls, almost fondling them. He set the cyclic pitch control, and the gleaming green-and-white machine lifted off the Tullahoma airstrip.

Gail took one last look at the cluster of well-wishers gathered on the tarmac, well away from the rotor-blade wash. Tom and Monica still wore their wedding attire—at that distance, Gail had an eerie feeling that she was looking at Alex and herself.

A short distance away, Joe waited with Dorie, who still wore a cast on her right arm. Gail's friend Alicia was with them, hugging herself in the chilly, late-autumn breeze, her orchid maid of honor's dress billowing silkily. Gail watched with interest as Walt slipped out of his tuxedo jacket and draped it over Alicia's shoulders.

The helicopter banked gently to the left, making a wide circle around the gathering. Gail waved one last time, unsure whether they could see her. A lump filled her throat as they waved back.

Then Alex raised the pitch control stick for more lift, and the chopper nosed down briefly, before setting off on a southeasterly heading. Gail leaned back in the straight seat and closed her eyes, soaking up a feeling of exhilarating freedom.

In a few weeks she would be returning to L.A. to complete the propulsion project at Martindale. She didn't look forward to the temporary separation from Alex, nor to the eventual severance of working ties with her old mentor, Dr. Calcutt. For the moment, however, all that seemed far away.

"Did it go all right?" Alex asked, raising his voice over the sound of the engine.

"Don't you know?"

Gail smiled at him, bemused. He had loosened his tie and traded his formal coat for a worn leather flight jacket, which made him look rakishly elegant.

Alex shook his head. "My eyes were too full of you to see anything else. You're the most beautiful bride in the history of the universe."

"It was a double wedding, my love," Gail reminded him. "Monica and I dressed and looked exactly alike."

Alex groaned. "I can't believe you two spent a week in L.A. together and came back with identical wardrobes."

"Be patient with us. We're going through a phase that we missed out on as children. Besides, we made a pact to never play tricks on you and Tom."

"You couldn't if you wanted to." Alex laughed. "Not anymore. During this past month, Tom and I have discovered that you and Monica are identically different. Take the honeymoons, for example. Monica chose two weeks of cruise-ship parties and island-hopping in the Caribbean. You prefer to go off to the boonies with hiking boots and goose-down jackets."

Gail smiled to herself, thinking about the French lace negligee that Alex didn't know about. Hiking in the woods around Pinehaven certainly appealed to her, but so did candlelight and soft music.

Clouds that had begun building in the west earlier in the day finally overtook the sun, cutting the glare on the helicopter's canopy. A line of shadow raced across the ragged treetops below.

"Dorie and Joe are engaged," she said. When Alex looked surprised, she added, "It happened this morning. I think they got carried away with our double wedding."

She could tell Alex was mulling that new situation. Gail wondered if they were thinking the same thing: love could survive a lot of punishment—and guilt. Of course, it hadn't hurt that Joe had practically camped out at the hospital during Dorie's entire stay.

Gail fingered the thin gold bracelet that Alicia had loaned her—the "something borrowed" for the traditional wedding. Once Alicia had gotten over the shock of seeing Gail and Monica seated together in the Venetian Room, she had plunged into their wedding plans like a third sister. She had flown out to Tullahoma three days early, more or less taking charge, until she'd eventually butted heads with Walt. The pair had seemed an absurd mismatch at the wedding, with Walt threatening to burst the seams of his rented tux. Ordinarily strong-willed and almost predatory around men, Alicia had appeared to be strangely buffaloed by the burly Shadow technician.

"Are you upset over Walt insisting on being best man?" Gail asked.

Alex considered that for a moment and shook his head. "He started off just trying to horn in, so he could work off his grudge against me. But in a crazy sort of way, we all ended up feeling like a family again. That suits me fine."

Gail reached over and laid a hand on his, as Alex made slight adjustments to the helicopter's controls.

She had never known a man who had such a deep yearning for family.

She had been nervous about Alex piloting them to Pinehaven, considering his hair-raisingly absent-minded driving technique on the ground. But he seemed sublimely at home in the air, in total unity with aircraft and sky.

Tears formed in her eyes as they climbed higher into the Appalachian Mountains, crossing the un-seen boundary between Tennessee and North Caro-lina. She caught herself watching for Pinehaven long before the Smokies came into view in the distance.

Pinehaven reminded her of something she hadn't intended to dredge up now. But the need to clear the question from the back of her mind suddenly seemed all-important.

"Alex," she said hesitantly, "I have to ask you about the portrait you painted—of Monica."

His expression didn't change. After awhile, though, he took a deep breath and blew it out through pursed lips.

"I didn't know you'd seen that, sweetheart," he said finally. "It must have shocked you."

Gail watched his face closely, uncertain as to what she was looking for. In her heart of hearts she knew this was a subject that she had always been afraid of touching.

"I'm not sure how to explain it," Alex said, "except to say that the portrait isn't of Monica—it's of you."

"Me?" Her hand tightened on his. "But you didn't even know I existed when you painted it."

He smiled wistfully. "Oh, you existed. I've carried you around inside me for a long, long time."

He glanced at her, and his expression grew serious. "I was never in love with Monica, sweetheart. Not for one second. But when I sat down to paint a portrait of my ideal woman, I realized she would look just like Monica. Only she wouldn't *be* like Monica.

"Being just a fantasy, I could make her anything I wanted her to be. So she would look like Monica and—heart and soul—*be* like no one I'd ever known." He glanced at her again, a little shyly. "My fantasy would be just like you."

Gail smiled back at him. She ran her fingertips over his high cheekbones and across his lips, where they received a kiss.

The cloud cover had lowered. Alex followed the landmarks, guiding the little Bell toward home. A gossamer ribbon of snowflakes had begun collecting around the edges of the bubble cockpit. He set the throttle wide open, racing the storm. When he saw the familiar curl of the French Broad River, then the peak of the cedar-shingled roof atop his mountain, he knew he had won.

He flew low over the cabin, smiling down at the smoke wafting from the chimney. As usual, Rafe had come through for him. Alex was confident that Rafe had followed the rest of his instructions to the letter, most likely adding a few embellishments of his own.

The special dinner that Alex had ordered from the restaurant down in Brevard would be waiting in the preset microwave oven. There would be two place settings on the low table before the hearth, with a bottle of champagne cooling in an ice bucket.

The portrait upstairs in the master bedroom slipped back into his thoughts. Alex smiled inwardly. The wall that he had always thought existed between dreams and reality had blurred and grown indistinct. He sighed softly and allowed his dreams free rein.

Now he was standing in front of the crackling fire. He pulled Gail into his arms, teasing her lips with the softest of kisses. The coat slipped from her shoulders and fell to the floor. Slowly he unbuttoned her blouse as she held her wineglass to his lips. Then she reached up and worked the knot out of his tie before unbuttoning his shirt and baring his chest to her kisses. Snow lashed the windows, but they were warm—so warm in the rosy firelight.

"Look, there's Rafe!" Gail cried, pointing down, interrupting his reverie.

Alex circled the helicopter around the clearing, grinning. Rafe stood at the edge of the new landing pad, frantically waving both arms. The landing lights ringing the pad glowed red, and festive red and white streamers fluttered from the branches of the trees surrounding the clearing.

As Alex skillfully maneuvered the helicopter over the pad, Gail gasped. Painted in the center of the landing pad were two perfect roses, tied together with a red ribbon. Alex spotted them at the same moment and laughed appreciatively.

"I suppose that's Rafe's wedding present to us," he commented.

"Oh, Alex," Gail said, waving at Rafe. "I think I'm falling in love with that boy."

SILHOUETTED against the firelight in the pine-scented living room, Gail felt light-headed as Alex poured their first glass of sparkling wine. He bent to kiss her, and her coat fell to the floor at their feet.

Slowly, slowly, he unbuttoned her blouse while sipping from the wineglass that she held to his lips. She drew the knot from his tie, unbuttoned his shirt, and pressed her lips to his quivering chest.

Snow lashed the windows. She felt a warm glow rising within her. He lowered her to the thick rug in front of the crackling fire, their lips came together, and she felt him smile. They soared over their own horizon.

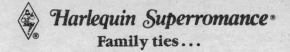

Harlequin Superromance®
Family ties...

SEVENTH HEAVEN
In the introduction to the Osborne family trilogy,
Kate Osborne finds her destiny with Police
Commissioner Donovan Cade.

Available in December

ON CLOUD NINE
Kate's second daughter, Juliet, has old-fashioned
values like her mother's. But those values are tested
when she meets Ross Stafford, a jazz musician,
sometime actor and teaching assistant . . . and the
object of her younger sister's affections. Can Juliet
only achieve her heart's desire at the cost of her
integrity?

Coming in January

SWINGING ON A STAR
Meridee is Kate's oldest daughter, but very much her
own person. Determined to climb the corporate
ladder, she has never had time for love. But her life is
turned upside down when Zeb Farrell storms into
town determined to eliminate jobs in her company—
her sister's among them! Meridee is prepared to do
battle, but for once she's met her match.

Coming in February

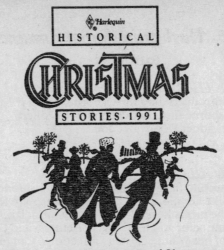

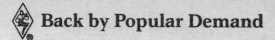

Back by Popular Demand

Janet Dailey
Americana

A romantic tour of America through fifty favorite Harlequin Presents, each set in a different state researched by Janet and her husband, Bill. A journey of a lifetime in one cherished collection.

In January, don't miss the exciting states featured in:

Title #23 **MINNESOTA**
Giant of Mesabi

#24 **MISSISSIPPI**
A Tradition of Pride

Available wherever Harlequin books are sold.

JD-JAN

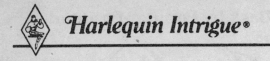

Harlequin Intrigue®

Trust No One...

When you are outwitting a cunning killer, confronting dark secrets or unmasking a devious imposter, it's hard to know whom to trust. Strong arms reach out to embrace you—but are they a safe harbor...or a tiger's den?

When you're on the run, do you dare to fall in love?

For heart-stopping suspense and heart-stirring romance, read Harlequin Intrigue. Two new titles each month.

HARLEQUIN INTRIGUE—where you can expect the unexpected.

fir. —3.00